MINISTERS

with

WHITE COLLARS

and

BLACK SECRETS

Deborah Smith

Deborah Smith Publications
Union, New Jersey

Deborah Smith is available for speaking engagements.
Contact:
Renaissance Management Service
P.O. Box 548
New York, NY 10031
(866) 317-5552 Office
(212) 368-5228 Fax

Ministers With White Collars And Black Secrets

Cover Design by:
Vizuri Designs - Danielle Pettiford

Editor:
Terre L. Holmes & Krista M. Harman

ISBN:0-9746136-0-6

1051 Stuyvesant Avenue, # 319
Union, NJ 07083
www.deborahsmithonline.com

Dedication

To my Lord and Savior Jesus Christ: *'Your grace and mercy have truly brought me through. I'm living this moment because of you.'* In you I have found myself, and through you I will continue to edify humanity while glorifying Your name. Your praise will always be in my mouth and in my writing.

To my children, Kindness and TJ: When I look at all of the gifts that God has given me, you both by far are my greatest treasures. I live to be an example of how you can achieve any dream, no matter how big. I love you unceasingly and unconditionally.

In memory of my dear Mother, Evangelist Constance B. Smith: Neither words nor deeds could ever express the admiration and appreciation to my Lord and Savior Jesus Christ for giving me the gift of life through such an awesome woman of God. Mommy, I Love You.

To my Dad, Bishop Willie L. Smith Sr.: You are and always will be the most respected businessman I know. Thank you for being the type of father that most men can only aspire to be. I will always believe in you because you've always given me reasons to, time and time again. I love you.

To my Brothers and Sisters, Willie, Victor, Bernard, Lori, Jerry and Tyrone: Thanks for all of your support throughout the writing of this book, as well as all of my life's endeavors. Being the baby sure has its perks when you are blessed with siblings like you.

To my Sister, Roberta: You hold an extra special place in my heart in that you have been like a second mother to me; even more, my best friend. Thank you for your encouragement, guidance and commitment. I could not have found the peace of mind to release this project without your faith in it.

To the love of my life, Dy-Shawn Simpkins: Though there may be rain, you are the sunshine and serenity that has helped this flower to bloom. I only hope to match the dedication to our life and love that you have shown to me and the world. The air is so sweet when you are around. Everything is coming up roses!

Acknowledgements

I am deeply appreciative to all of the wonderful people who have help make this book possible.

A Heartfelt Thanks To:

Lisa and Julian Wilson of Renaissance Management Service. Lisa, thank you for believing in me and for being the force to help me to release this novel with clarity professionalism, and expertise. And to Julian, for being so generous in lending such a wonderful, gifted, talent and exceptional women to me.

To Danielle Pettiford of Vizuri Designs. Your special gift has brought my dream to life; live and in living color!

To Terré Holmes, a very gifted and visionary editor.

To Hasani Pettiford for your support and encouraging words. You have mentored me through this process.

To Tu-Shonda Whitaker, Gloria Burgess, Beverly Smith and Vanessa Johnson for all your help in reading and re-reading, and re-reading this story.

To my sister Lori Anderson, because your *'crazy faith'* can move mountains, and your testimony encourages even the least of them.

To my brother, Minister Jerry Smith, I write volumes because I am inspired through your preaching, and the anointing and power God has given you through your ministry.

To my friends, church family and loved ones, because I have received the greatest amount of prayers and support from you!

Foreword

Ministers with White Collars and Black Secrets is definitely an eye opening experience for people who have had to deal with the lies and deceptions within the ranks of ministry. The novel's main character, Kiyah, delivers a true message of victory to those who believe that deliverance and peace will be found in their relationship with God.

Deborah is a successful black woman who has achieved balance in both the spiritual and professional aspects of her life. Her life's experiences are a testament to her strength and vitality. She embodies the biblical definition of a '*Virtuous Woman, for her price is far above rubies.*' There is no doubt in my mind that what you read in this novel will stick with you for a lifetime.

It gives me great honor to pen this forward and to wish Deborah the best in her endeavor to open up to us the great wealth of information that God has deposited in her, through the testimony of her trials. May God continue to bless you Deb, and make your way in life easy and successful.

Yours because of Christ

Pastor Terrell Turner
New Vision International Ministry Inc.
Newark, N.J.

Chapter One

Starting Over

It was a crisp, clear summer day. I woke up this morning expecting something magical to happen. You see, my heart had just begun to heal from the deep wounds of my failed marriage to Michael. Six months ago, I would have never thought that everything and everyone would look vibrant and alive to me once again. Michael - I like to refer to him as Mr. Man who thought he had the master plan. Well his plan had worked for a while, fifteen long years to be exact. I had been with Michael for three years and married to him for twelve. Michael was good at controlling someone's mind. He knew how to talk people into believing what he wanted them to believe. He definitely had the gift of gab. He loved women, and every time he was suspected of going outside of our relationship his defense would be, "You made me" or "It's all your fault, if you would have did this or did that, I would never have ventured off." Yeah right. Michael was just a dog. Just when he knew that I was totally finished with him and was completely fed up, he would use his secret weapon. I can see Michael now playing his, "I'm in trouble" Christian music. Then he would start being so family orientated, concerned and unusually considerate. Michael knew that I had deep spiritual beliefs and he would use that to his advantage by throwing God into the picture and quoting scriptures on *how the woman should be submissive to the husband* and *how the husband is the head.* He never read further down in the scripture to the part about how a man should provide for his house as the head and how the man should also cleave unto his own wife and not every other woman in town. I did not realize that then, but I sure do now. He wanted to be the head, but, he didn't want to pay any bills.

Damn, I was really stupid and naïve! After all, I was a virgin when we met. He was my first and I intended for him to be my last. My mother always instilled in me to keep myself for my husband and God would bless our union. Well, fifteen years later, I'm still waiting on that *blessing.* Back to Mr. Man; he would start talking about God and how lucky he was to have me. See, he knew that by talking as if he was saved once again, I would soften and give him another chance. But, oh no, not this time. He had sung that song one too many times for me. I had to, for once, think of myself and *my* happiness. I always found a reason to try

12

to make it work. You know, the kids, the house, and more importantly what people might say. It was sad to think about the fact that my life long love, my destiny, my husband had betrayed me. I guess I felt victimized.

I called the cops because Mr. Man said that he was not going to leave HIS HOUSE. Did this man fall into stupid? *His house?* What mortgage did he ever pay? More importantly, what type of man would even fathom his wife and two children being uprooted and inconvenienced? What type of man? I'll tell you what type of man, Mr. Man with the master plan. But he had another thing coming this time. I got myself a restraining order, changed the locks on our quarter of a million dollar home and told his sorry ass never to return again. After all, if he wanted to play the field he shouldn't be limited to just playing there, let him and his master plan LIVE THERE. Did I fail to mention that I also worked two jobs, paid his car note as well as the note for my brand new Mercedes E 430? Bought his Armani suits, as well as my Dana Buckman dresses and suits. He only wore the most expensive clothes and only Enyce and Sean John jeans. I, myself have a passion for Parasuco. They designed those jeans with me especially in mind. Now we were not the type of parents, that looked good and our kids did not. We kept it gangster and my daughter Kyaisa loved to look pretty. She is twelve and she knows those name brands as well as any adult. My son, Kaseem, now he's just eight but he likes new clothes. He doesn't care so much

13

about the name just as long as they are new. However, when it comes to his footwear, that's a different story. He will only wear Air Force One sneakers and only Timberland boots will do. We have good kids, and they have their little sneaky ways like most kids. But over all I thank God that they are healthy and reasonably good.

So, getting back to Liberation Day. You know the day I closed the final curtain on Mr. Man. He was so angry, he called me everything but a child of God. What happened to his salvation that day? *He* screwed up and had the nerve to be mad at me. I guess he thought for one obscure moment that he would be able to run around with women on me, and would still be able to maintain his lavish lifestyle that *I* provided. Stay with me. He wore Versace shoes, custom made furs, and drove around in an eighty thousand dollar vehicle and did not work *anywhere*. Just to make sure you didn't miss that, THE MAN DID NOT WORK ANYWHERE. Let me explain.

I was a brand new fool, riding down the street on roller skates wearing a Bozo the Clown outfit. I didn't know any better. I thought as a Christian woman, this was the right thing to do. Support my man. Submit myself to my husband. Mr. Man's famous speech would always get me; you know the one about how he took care of me when we first met. Well that was twelve years ago. We had been together for fifteen years, have two children and he had been pimping me for far too long. But let me get back to

14

this cool, crisp summer day.

Anyway, it was the first really warm day of the year. My sisters and I, along with some friends, decided to play hooky from work and go shopping in Manhattan. After all, my sister Robin, we all call her "Queen Bee", is the boss. She's a very conscientious business woman who doesn't take any stuff. Although she's all business at work, when it comes to family she has a heart of gold. She is truly my best friend. Ever since our dear mother passed two years ago, she has stepped in and been just what our family needs to survive. Robin is a very beautiful woman inside and out; our Indian heritage definitely shows up in her features. Queen Bee, could have been further ahead by now, if she wasn't so generous, but that's just how she is. She loves the Lord and she loves helping people, especially me. She also loves her diamonds and she wears fabulous jewelry. She has all her jewelry custom made at Z & L Jewelry Store in our town. Even her everyday jewelry would make jaws drop wide open. I love my sister dearly; she has been my rock throughout my most troublesome times.

Anyway back to the shopping trip. It was myself, Queen Bee, my sister Ever Ready (I call her Ever Ready because she is forever ready to fight). She has a quick temper and is easily offended. Ironically, she is the quiet one in the family. Ever Ready looks a lot like me, she's six years older and in good shape. She's very sweet, but just don't rub her the wrong way. Ever

Ready is a good cook. Both my sisters can throw down, but Ever Ready's macaroni and cheese is anointed. I just have to say, "Thank You Jesus", because His presence shows up in that macaroni and cheese. Sister Thomas and Sister Darlene also came along with us. Now these two were my sister Queen Bee's cut buddies. They were loyal members of my father's church. I meant to say, they are loyal members of God's church of which my father is the pastor. My Dad always reminds us of that fact. "This is God's church," my Dad would adamantly say. My Dad, Bishop Dr. Dean Pastor Winston Simmons, is truly a man of God. He is a testimony of the unlimited power of God. He had only completed the sixth grade in school and God with His awesome power had enabled him to become the founder of the very first Bible College in New Jersey.

Furthermore, he has gone on to open forty-six extension schools throughout the country. Moreover, my Dad (I like the way that sounds) started his church in the basement of our childhood home of which he still lives in, twenty-four years ago with just his wife, eight children and Sister Betty Haynes from our previous church, Ecclesiastics Church of Christ. He has since built a five million dollar facility and put over half down in cash. Only God can take nothing and make something out of it.

Now, after myself, Robin, Ever Ready, Sister Thomas and Sister Darlene had finished shopping, we decided to eat in downtown Newark at John's Place. John's Place is a restaurant where everybody who is somebody in our area goes to eat. It's an elegant, warm, and inviting place to eat and the food tastes like somebody's grandmother cooked it. The *only* problem is, you just have to worry about whether your car will still be outside when you finish eating. I was a little reluctant about going to John's today, because I was not particularly dressed to impress at the time. However, since everyone else really had a taste for John's fried chicken and collard greens, I didn't want to be a party pooper.

So we went to John's and of course, just as I feared, I ran into several people I knew. I should have known better. I lived in Newark all of my life, on the same block, in the same house, with the same telephone number. To make matters worse, I have five brothers, two sisters, twenty-seven nieces and nephews and six great nieces and nephews *and* my father is the pastor of one of the biggest churches in our area. It is almost impossible for me to go anywhere locally and not run into somebody I know.

After I said my hellos and made small talk, I finally sat down with my party to order my late lunch. As usual, even though I was looking 'hit', I did catch the eye of a few admirers. There was nothing really special about any of them, so I just acted like I didn't notice their gestures. I had just gotten out of a bad relationship and was finally enjoying being by myself. But as I was halfway through my fried fish dinner with yams and cabbage, I looked up and looked across at the next table. There were three men having what appeared to be a very intense business

17

meeting/lunch type of thing going on. Two were average looking men. But there was something different about the other one. He wore a sweat suit, but it wasn't just a sweat suit. It was pure white and very expensive, you could just tell from the look of the material. I was an expert when it comes to these sorts of things. He complimented his sweat suit with a pure white leather baseball cap that was neatly placed in his lap, and his sneakers were Gucci, without the G's splattered all over them. Seeing as though I have radar for these types of things, it wasn't hard for me to spot them. I'll admit, I was shocked to see a *Black Man* wearing Gucci sneakers, without the G's all over them or at least a G' standing out somewhere so that everybody would know that he spent $385 for them. I was totally beside myself at that point. This was a step up from flossing, this was what you call class! I was impressed, and trust me I am very hard to impress. This man was wearing those sneakers because he liked the finer things in life. He wasn't trying to inform everyone of his status by flaunting labels. *Wow*! A clean cut, well dressed black man, dressed well and looking good! '*I hear you Lord. Speak to me loud and clear.*' I said to myself. He was inspiring me to get up out my seat, run home, hop into my *Check Me Out* gear and bring some noise down to John's Place. But wait, it gets better. As I was watching him I noticed the jewelry. Now mind you, he wasn't the type of man who would normally catch my eye. You see I like a thuggish type of guy, but he has to possess some class; it's really interesting the way I see my perfect man. I like a tough, but gentle man. He can't be a punk, but then again he can't be a troublemaker. I'm a business-type, reserved sort of woman. I'm refined and I can also get ghetto when the atmosphere calls for it. However I tend to like attributes in a man that are so opposite of my own. Hey, they say opposites attract! This guy really had caught my attention. There were qualities in him that I had never seen all in one man at the same time, at least, in living color. Of course you see them on TV or in videos. That was it! He reminded me of Puff Daddy! Now Puff Daddy is my ideal man, he is an astute businessman, he can be thugged out and have so much class at the same time. Being as though the brother is fine and financially secure doesn't hurt much either.

Let's get back to the jewelry on this guy at John's Place. See ladies, it's those intricate details you must pay close attention to. Watch my analysis, I reviewed *everything* from head to toe to reach my conclusion. Oh my God! His necklace was platinum, not silver, not white gold; it was platinum with a cross medallion hanging from it made out of pure ice. Both items together cost anywhere between fifteen to twenty thousand dollars. Trust me I know these types of things. His ring was a cross made out of princess cut diamonds, and it sat glittering against his sand-colored complexion on his right middle finger. Pay close attention ladies, his right not left middle finger, which to me was a clear indication that he was not married. He had an iced out link bracelet to complete his look and a Rolex watch on his left wrist that loosely fit. His jewelry was impressive, but the most intriguing thing about him was the shrewd, alluring, mystical type of demeanor he demonstrated, while talking with the men at his table. This man definitely aroused my curiosity. You could just tell that his style was not something he acquired, but it was a way of life, of which he had always been accustomed to. My conclusion ladies is that the man had money and had it more abundantly.

While my family and friends were just rambling on, I, on the other hand, was engrossed in his activities, his movements, and doing my best to eavesdrop on his conversation, discreetly of course. Twice, I caught him looking at me. So, quite naturally, I decided to go to the ladies room. I wanted to give him the opportunity to get a full-length view. As I walked by his table, I could see through the mirrors on the wall that he stopped mid-conversation to glance over and look at me from top to bottom. On my way back to my table he nodded his head and smiled at me. I smiled back. Before I could sit down good Sister Thomas leaned over and said to me "Girl I think he likes you." I responded by saying "Please, Sister Thomas, I'm not thinking about him or any other man right now. My mind is stayed on the Lord." A good response coming from the pastor's daughter. But in my mind I'm thinking *'Lord, let this man approach me. Pleeeeeease Jesus!'*

This man had a smile that could melt a block of ice in five seconds flat. I figured him to be a drug dealer, but not the type of drug dealer that hung out on corners. If he was a drug dealer he seemed like the type that would only participate in very huge transactions. Maybe he is a lawyer, or even a very successful businessman, or maybe he was in the entertainment industry. I don't know, but one thing's for sure, the man had money. So as I continued to dab at my food, for which I really had lost my appetite, my god brother Kareem, who happens to be one of the chefs at John's Place, came out of the kitchen to greet me. We hugged and had small talk, while everyone at my table was finishing up and putting together their money for the bill. You know how we get when it's time to pay the bill. Ever Ready, the ring leader, with her big mouth, was like, "Please don't forget to add your tax in. You can't just take the price off the menu and think that's all you owe." I'm thinking, *'no she ain't trying to cramp my style, acting all ghetto in front of this classy man.'* She makes me sick. Every time we go out she gets into a fight or argument. One time on Father's Day the whole family went to Red Lobster and Ms. Every Ready gets into a fight with my oldest niece, Chocolate, over something stupid - I mean a physical fight, and to make matters worse some of our church members were in the restaurant to witness this. Well they had to call the police and everything. Let me tell you, I was so embarrassed that I just had to leave. Queen Bee was just fit to be tied. Chocolate is her daughter and ironically she is close to her Aunt Ever Ready. But you just have to be careful with Ever Ready; she will make a mountain out of a molehill. Anyway, back to the ruckus over the bill at John's Place. I was just looking at Ever Ready; wanting to slide her head to the other end of the restaurant. She just makes me so sick sometimes. *Why?* Why did she have to start her mess today? Not while this classy man was making a strong impression on me. Now that she had embarrassed me to no end, I had to revive my status. So I reached over and grabbed the bill out of Ever Ready's hand and at the same time giving her a look that said, 'Don't try me today sister. I *am* the one to diffuse your battery.' Her eyes got as big as the ceiling. She looked like she wanted a pound for pound match, but before she could say anything, Queen Bee jumped up and took her outside to talk to her. When my sister says 'let's go', you go. I don't know what Queen Bee said to Ever Ready when she took her outside, but when she came back in her battery was on low. That was a relief. I love my sister, but I'll bust her in the head in a New York minute. That's how my family is, we can fight each other and in two minutes it's like nothing ever happened. Don't get it twisted, we can fight or talk about each other all day, but we don't allow anyone else to try it.

I pulled out my Gold Corporate American Express Card and gave it to Ever Ready along with the bill and said, "I'll take care of the bill. You guys leave the tip." Now of course this made me look good, but in my spirit I was sick. I was thinking, '*Lord you know all about my $155 cable bill, and that Gucci hat and bag I bought from Short Hills Mall earlier this week that I don't have* *the money for. But you said in Your word that You shall supply all of my needs and wants (I just added that). Now work Lord Jesus and I hope you move before my next American Express bill comes.*' I had to exercise a little faith. I don't know what possessed those people to come up with a credit card that has to be paid in full every month. Now you know that ain't nothing but the Devil. This scene with the bill and all that, stifled my game plan, so I exited the restaurant.

I wasn't in the mood for being flirtatious, I just wanted to go get my kids and go home and get some much-needed rest. Every Ready had worked my last nerve. We headed towards my father's church, which is always our meeting spot. Once we finally got to the church, which was only about ten minutes away, we hugged, kissed and parted ways. I decided to go see my accountant on Clinton Avenue to go over my investments. Let me stop lying. I needed to dip into some of the very few certificate of deposits I had left. I was broke. My estranged husband had drained me dry. He really knew how to spend money. It was always something with Mr. Man; most people try to come up with money to pay their bills, Mr. Man would come up with bills to inspire him to spend money he had yet to obtain. *'Lord I thank You. You brought me out of darkness into the marvelous light.'* Anyway, as I was driving up Clinton Avenue my cell phone rang and my caller ID showed a number I did not recognize. At first I decided not to answer it. But finally after the third ring I

23

answered. "Hello, may I speak to Kiyah" a very distinctive and sexy voice said. I'm thinking, 'Hmmm, very good for a bill collector'.

I said, "This is she. Who may I ask is calling?"

The voice replied, "This is Mr. Booker."

Confused I said, "Mr. Booker? I'm not familiar with the name."

He interrupted me and said, "I'm sorry, but I saw you at John's Place earlier and I petitioned your god brother for a way of contacting you and he gave me this number. I hope that's okay with you." I was speechless. Instantly I knew it was the man that I had been so easily captivated by earlier today. He continued by saying, "Do you know who I am?"

I said, "No, I don't have a clue." He went on to describe where he was sitting and what he had on. Finally, I said, "Oh, yes I know who you are." Even though I knew all along, I couldn't let the man know I had been checking him out all the time. "What can I do for you?" I added.

"You can start by assuring me that it's okay that I called you this afternoon," he said rather smoothly.

"It's okay Mr. Booker, but how can I be of service to you?" I asked.

"Don't tempt me. It all depends on whether or not you're willing to honor *all* my requests," he said.

"I don't know about *all* of your request, but maybe I can

help you with something," I snapped back. "Please excuse my candor Kiyah. It's just that you're so beautiful, a man can't help but fantasize, but I'm a very respectable person and I would never insult you in any way."

Boy, was he smooth. "No, you didn't offend me Mr. Booker, but don't let it happen again," I said.

He laughed. "You have some funny friends. Especially the one with the big eyes." He was referring to Ever Ready. "That's my sister. I'm so embarrassed, I'm sorry you had to witness that." I said.

"Don't be, you can tell that you guys really love each other, and it looks like you guys really have a good time together" he said.

I thought that was nice of him to say, *and* it was true. "Yeah, you're right and I appreciate that," I said. As fate and my cheap cell phone would have it, my reception was really getting bad. It was so bad, to the point where he couldn't understand a word I was saying. I could hear him, but he couldn't hear me. Instead of going to see my accountant, I decided to head back to the church. Just as I reached the church, my reception came back, and I told him to call me at my office inside the church. We had a very pleasant conversation, and what I derived from the short time we talked was that he was extremely intelligent and very eloquent. Wow! They don't manufacturer men like this anymore. During the course of the conversation we joked about my cell phone and he even offered to buy me a better one. I'm thinking, 'Now this is my kind of man'. See it's not just good enough that he has the cash; he's got to like spending it on me. So far he was off to a good start. We talked for approximately thirty minutes, and then he mentioned he had to go to a meeting. *Hmm*, a meeting? Very impressive. He promised to call me back as soon as he finished. I knew that I would be leaving the office soon, so I told him to try me on my cell phone.

I did some follow up work at the office and gossiped with my sister-in-law, Benita, my oldest brother Wali's wife. Benita is a very sweet lady and very attractive at forty-nine. She has a full head of gray hair, but her features are so soft it doesn't age her at all. Benita is very fair skin and approximately a size 20 but very shapely. You can't tell her she ain't cute. She's very professional and has excellent people skills. She is definitely good for business. But she is so nosy. She wants to know everything. She will stay up till dawn to get some good gossip. She's not just the average nosy person; she wants details. I mean real intricate details, like the questions she asked me about my encounter with Mr. Booker. Her interrogation went something like this: "What did he have on? What color was it? When did he look at you? How did he look at you? What did you do when he looked at you? How many steps did he take towards you? Which foot did he step with first?" Oh My God! Benita is the real live Inspector Gadget of Gossip. But, I must say, she really cares about people and you can be sure that she will keep your secrets to herself. I love her because she is always there when I need someone to talk to.

After gossiping with Benita, I mean, being interrogated by Benita, I picked the kids up from Queen Bee's house. Her house is like a mini-mansion, with five bathrooms, two decks, a huge backyard, big screen televisions everywhere, even in her garage. The entire house was lavishly furnished. She had all of her furniture imported directly from Italy. My kids love being over there. So after gathering up their things, I finally drag the kids to the car and headed home. Once we got to my house, which is only six minutes away from my sister, I start to prepare dinner.

It was one of those days that called for a quick meal, especially since I wasn't even hungry. I fried some wing flings, made a salad with boiled eggs, croutons and Parmesan cheese and gave the kids corn on the cob on the side. It took me all of twenty-five minutes to have dinner on the table. Corn on the cob is Kaseem's favorite. Fried chicken is Kyaisa's favorite. They both love salad so I was batting a thousand with this meal. They loved it and I loved the convenience.

After eating, the kids took their showers and prepared for bed. After tucking them in, I went into my room and put on my Yolanda Adams CD and as the tunes of *Open My Heart* filled the room I started thinking about everything I've been through in the past two years; my mother's painful death, the break up of my marriage and I know I have a lot of bitterness inside of me. I

27

started talking to the Lord, '*Lord, You know this situation has put me in a state where I don't trust men. Lord, this situation has me to the point that when I go to church I leave feeling empty. I feel so burdened, like I can't praise You. Lord I need Your guidance. Maybe I need to start considering a saved man, a godly man. I don't know why I can't bring myself to get involved with a minister or deacon. I'm just not attracted to them. Lord, they seem so erratic, always throwing the Word at you, even on dates. There is a time and place for everything. Nobody wants to be rebuked for wearing jeans to a movie or having red nail polish on their toes. I know that Your Word says "how can two walk together except they be one?", so Lord send me a man that loves You, a saved man, but one that can love me and not try to make me a missionary. And Lord I don't want no stiff old deacon or minister. Lord, I need to hear from You.*" My conversation with God was interrupted when my cell phone rang, I recognize the number, it was Mr. Booker.

"Hello" I answered.

"Kiyah" he said with his distinctive voice.

"Yes, this is she. Whom may I ask is calling" I said, even though I knew it was him all along. I couldn't for one minute let him think that I was checking for him like that.

"This is Mr. Booker, sweetheart, I wanted to keep my word and call you back after I finished with my meeting," he said and then paused for a minute and continued. "And Kiyah, I was anxious to hear your voice again."

First of all I wasn't his sweetheart, but hey I liked his style. The man sure was smooth. "Really, that's nice of you to say," I replied. I hadn't heard that one before.

He then said, "Maybe we can go out to lunch tomorrow, and get better acquainted; where ever you would like to go?"

"Maybe", I replied, "but there are a few things I need to know."

"Feel free sweetheart, ask me anything you like," he said confidently.

So, I began my third degree. "Are you married?" I asked.

"No, but I was. I have two children, my son is seventeen and my daughter is twelve."

Okay, I'm thinking, he must be old. I'm thirty-two and I don't want no old man. Since he answered my second question about whether or not he had kids, I decided to throw another one in there. "How old are you?" I asked.

He replied proudly, "Thirty-nine. Why, is that too old for you?"

"Of course not," I answered. Really it was, but hey it's a free meal, and I don't have anything else better to do. Besides this guy was rather intriguing.

He then says, "Listen, Kiyah, it doesn't take more than three or four dates to know whether or not we want to be committed."

Whoa! Slow down Tonto. He was jumping the gun. I

thought, 'this man is crazy'. "Listen, Mr. Booker, I don't know about you, but I don't make those type of decisions after three or four dates." He adamantly explained that he could tell if he wanted to be committed to someone in three or four dates. Okay, I could see right away why he was single and had no serious relationship, because he was just too hasty at making important decisions. He looked good, and was very intelligent, but he moved entirely too fast. I knew right then that this was not going to work. Anyway, I wasn't interested in a relationship with him. I just asked God to send me a saved man, a godly man and he was definitely not that. He had to be someone that God was just using to tie me over until he located my ideal companion. So I accepted his invitation for lunch the next day. Who knew, maybe we could be the best of friends.

After a few more minutes, I politely told him that I was going to be retiring for the evening. I got off the phone and dived into my closet to find an outfit for the following day. After a half an hour of trying on clothes, I realized that it was past ten o'clock. I took my shower and afterwards, I climbed right into bed, turned up the volume on my Yolanda Adams CD, which was still playing from earlier. She was now belting out track number ten "I need a blessing". It sounded like she was crying out to the Lord. Her words filled the room. ' I need a blessing, sinful though my heart may be. I need you to come down and bless me, even me Lord. I need you to stop by, not tomorrow, but today. I need a blessing

Jesus, even me, even me.' These were the last words I heard and for the first time in months I drifted off into a peaceful sleep.

Chapter Two

The Office

It was Tuesday morning and I woke up to the sounds of "Fresh Oil" which is a televised ministry by Bishop Noel Jones. I try to watch it every Tuesday morning at seven o'clock. The man can preach. I usually leave my television on that station the night before, so I don't forget. I felt that he was speaking directly to me that morning; his topic had something to do with being delivered but not healed. What a paradox - this was a revelation to me. I was delivered from the pain and stress of the break up of my marriage, but I was not healed. I realized this, every time I looked at my children and the hurt and sadness they must have felt from the loss of their father. He didn't come around and he didn't call often. This really bothers me, because when they are hurting, I am hurting. It breaks my heart to know that their little hearts are experiencing such grief. I'm still bitter and confused. I'm a nice looking young lady. I never cheated on my husband and I supported him in all of his failed ventures. I worked, paid my tithes, didn't drink, didn't smoke, didn't hang out and I was always willing to accommodate him in the bedroom. "The bedroom is undefiled," the Bible says. "A wife should submit herself to her husband." So why did he cheat? I just can't understand it. We had everything, businesses, houses, beautiful children, and a fairly wonderful life. As the tears began to fall, I looked into the mirror and said to myself, "Girl not today. Get yourself together. You don't need puffy eyes today. Hey! You never know, your healing may be waiting for you at lunch today."

Enough with the pity party. I got myself up and went into the bathroom, exfoliated my face and body, brushed my teeth, began doing my crunches for about five minutes on the bedroom floor. At the same time I was rushing the kids in and out of the bathroom. Once the kids were all done with the bathroom, I quickly took a two minute shower, dried off and rubbed my body down with some Victoria Secrets "Love Spell" lotion. Hey, a girl's got to do, what a girl's got to do. But to seal the deal, I decided to wear my *sock it to him* leopard jeans with a black fur vest and some black strappy sandals for fun. Then I took an additional five minutes to put on my face. I didn't wear a lot of make-up, just mascara, lip liner, lip gloss and eyeliner to add just a little bit more definition to my eyebrows. While the kids were getting their things and getting into the car, I looked into the full-length mirror on the back of my bedroom door. I turned to the back, "check", and then I turned to the right side, "check." I turned to the front, "check", then I turned to the left side, "check." Everything was looking good and in order. Okay, I was ready to go! Well, well, well, Mr. Booker, I wasn't dressed yesterday at John's Place, how ya like me now. I was looking good and feeling good that morning.

I locked up the house, set the alarm, hopped into my car, told the kids to put their seatbelts on, opened the glove compartment, where I kept the kids vitamins, gave each of them one, and then started my Mary, Mary CD. I had to thank God for my many blessings every morning; He has been so good to me. They used to sing a song when I was little about how God opened doors I could not see. Well, I didn't know then what that meant, but I do now. I don't know how I got to where I was on that day. I never thought I could handle all of this responsibility on my own. But I was not on my own, I had Jesus and he had carried me through the storms and I had no doubt that he would see me through many more. The first song on Mary, Mary's CD was *Thank You* and I just couldn't help but get emotional, especially when they got to the part that says "Where would I be without Your love, where would I be without Your grace, what would I have done if You hadn't come along, what would I have become,

You didn't have to do it, but I'm glad You did." God is so good. My eyes began to fill with water as I thought about how undeserving I was to have God intervene on my behalf in every manner of my life. He had went before me and made a way out of no way. He had given me peace when I had totally forgotten what it felt like. *'Lord I thank You, but Lord I still need a man.'*

This was my daily routine. The only difference that day was that I had a date. It was 7:40a.m. when I reached Kyaisa's school. "Okay, Kyaisa, have a good day. I love you."

She replied, "I love you too Mom, I need more money."

"For what!?" I asked, rather annoyed. Kyaisa quickly explained. "I want to go to the store after school with my friends."

"Okay Kyaisa here's another dollar." The girl thought I was made of money. We kissed and I had to go a few blocks up to drop Kaseem off at his school. Once we arrived at his school, he followed suit with "Mom can I have a dollar?"

"For what!?" I asked again, annoyed.

He replied, "I don't know. Kyaisa asked for one."

Hey, what could I say, at least he was honest. So I gave him a dollar too, kissed him, and told him to have a good day and I was off to work. I was traveling down highway seventy eight, thinking about what I might say, or what I might do in the presence of Mr. Booker at lunch. Every few seconds, I was practicing my smile in the rearview mirror. I was acting like I had never been on a date before. It really had been a long time. Ten minutes later, I pulled up to the office. I parked my car in the usual spot and as I got out the car, I noticed that it was a nice, clear day. I walked into the church, and as I passed some of the workers, they were ranting and raving about how nice I looked. Ms. Samuels said to me, "Ms. Kiyah, you must have a date, 'cause girlfriend you sure look good today."

"Thank you Ms. Samuels. I'm having lunch with a friend today. Just a friend." I was thinking if it was possible that Ms. Samuels already knew about my date. Then suddenly I remembered that I had spoken to Benita last night before I went to bed. That darn Benita, she just can't keep her mouth shut for one minute. She's just like and upset stomach, everything that goes in, comes out. I promised myself not to tell her anything else. As I approached the office where Benita was, I got my "tell her off speech" ready. But as soon as I hit the doorway, Benita yelled, "Girl, you betta work it!. You're gonna knock him off of his feet." She went on to say, "Those jeans are sharp."

"Thanks Benita. I sure hope so," I said.

Benita replied loudly, "Ain't no hope in it girlfriend, unless the man is blind, he is definitely going to be overwhelmed by you today." Benita was something else. She knew that she had ran her mouth all over the building, so what she was doing to smooth things over was to flatter me. Don't get me wrong, she was not (listen carefully) she was not exaggerating by any means. Now, watch this. Flattery will definitely get you <u>not</u> told off. Besides,

Benita is a good person and she means well. "Benita do me a favor, call the Manor and make reservations for two at noon please."

"The Manor," Benita screamed. "They charge at least a hundred dollars a plate."

"*And*, I'm worth it," I replied matter-of-factly. "Just do what I asked, Benita, thank you."

But, of course, Benita just had to keep going on and on about it. "Girl you are something else. How do you know that man can afford lunch at the Manor?" Benita asked.

By that time, I was annoyed. That darn Benita, she just had to relight my fire. Earlier she extinguished it with all of the flattery. I said, "Listen, Ms. Benita, since you gotta know everything, the man had on over thirty thousand dollars worth of jewelry. I am confident that he can pay for a $200 meal. He was flossing and now I'm checking him for the gloss. Anyway, he said he'd take me where ever I wanted to go, and I <u>want</u> <u>to</u> <u>go</u> to the Manor. So can you just make the reservations PLEASE?"

While Benita was making the reservations, I went to the ladies room to give Benita and the rest of the office staff a chance to talk about me and the performance I had just given them. I could just hear them now. "Oh, no she didn't. She thinks she's cute, and *she ain't saved* with those jeans on." They were by far stuck on stupid if they didn't think Benita wasn't going to record every word they said. <u>Watch</u> <u>this</u>; I said record every word *they* said, not what *she* says and replay it back to me later. It didn't bother me one bit. What didn't kill me could only make me stronger. Anyway, they talked about Jesus.

As I walked into the office, the same ones that were talking about me were all up in my face, asking me questions about my date. I put up the stop the bus sign with my hand and said, " I know ya'll was talking about me. Now ya'll all up in my business. I ain't got nothing to say." Everything got quiet for a minute and then we all started laughing. It's funny, because we did that to each other all of the time. The fact of the matter was we loved each other. Benita was the first one to say, "That's right, we were talking about you, 'cause you won't tell us nothing. What's up?" Benita's engine was running full speed ahead now. She continued, "What kind of work does he do? Where does he live? How old is he? Is he tall? Is he short? Is he light skin? Is he dark skin and bald headed? Girl ain't nothin' like a tall, dark and bald headed man..."

"Slow down Alex Trebek," I interrupted Benita. "I don't know all the answers to your questions, but I will find out in about twenty minutes and I will let you know."

Benita came right back at me with, "Call us from your cell phone." I couldn't believe how nosey Benita could be.

"I will not call you from my cell phone, *but* I will give you a detailed report when I return," I said with a wink. Benita has a sickness, a real live sickness, called nosiness! Well,

38

time flew. It was almost eleven o'clock, and he would be arriving in twenty minutes. I was getting a little nervous. It had been a while since I had been on a date. Oh, I said that already. I was just getting so nervous because in a matter of minutes he would be at my job and I was hoping that I looked okay. While I was standing there staring at Benita in pure amazement over her nosiness, Sandy yelled over to me, "Kiyah the phone's for you and his voice sure sounds familiar."

Sandy was a young lady that worked in our office. She had Benita beat when it came to gossip. She lived off of it. She knew everybody and their mama in every church. "*His voice?*" I replied in a very agitated tone.

"Oh! I'm sorry Kiyah. It's a "Mr. Booker" for you on line three," Sandy said with a puzzled look on her face. I was thinking, 'I know this fool is not calling to cancel on me twenty minutes before our lunch date.'

"Thank you, Sandy. Don't overload your brain trying to figure out who he is. You don't know him." Every now and then I had let her have it, because she was always dipping into my business. Benita is one thing. At least she is family. But Ms. Girl needed to understand her place, and her place was not in my business. I picked up line three " Hello, this is Kiyah."

"Hello, Kiyah, this is Mr. Booker and I just wanted to let you know, that I was so looking forward to our lunch date this afternoon," he said with that oh so distinctive voice of his.

"That's very sweet of you to say Mr. Booker, but we're scheduled to meet in approximately ten minutes. Are you going to be late or something? I thought you would call once you arrived near my area," I said, a little confused as to why he was calling.

"Oh, no sweetheart, there are certain engagements that just motivate me to be very punctual and this is one of them," he paused and continued. "Actually Kiyah, I just wanted to make sure you received the bouquet of flowers I sent you."

Severely confused I replied "A bouquet of flowers?" As I turned around to question the office staff with my eyes, a bouquet of flowers were being delivered by a delivery man. It was the most beautiful bouquet of wild flowers I had ever seen. It had orchids, lilies, sunflowers, roses and several other types of flowers I couldn't call by name. They were in all sorts of pastel colors and the vase was real crystal with a very elegant design. "Oh, my God, Mr. Booker, you didn't have to do that. They are so beautiful. Thank you. That was so sweet of you." I was, for once in my life, speechless.

"Kiyah," he said. "Of course I had to do that, it is just a token of my appreciation because you accepted my invitation for lunch on such short notice." Little did he know that his token was going to be in that bill for lunch he would be buying at the Manor that afternoon. but sending this beautiful bouquet of flowers right before our date was definitely first rate. This man had class and he was definitely smooth. "Mr. Booker, this is a pleasant surprise. I love flowers. Thanks so much," I said as my face lit up.

You're welcome," he said and continued, "I'm outside. It's twenty minutes to twelve. I don't want to rush you. Take your time, but while I'm waiting, why don't you give me the address to where you would like to eat so I can compute it into my navigation system." 'Hmm, *navigation system*? He must have an expensive car,' I thought. "Mr. Booker I was thinking about The Manor in West Orange, are you familiar with it?"

He quickly replied, "Yes, I am. I believe you have to make reservations in advance. Don't you think it may be too late to get them now?" he asked reluctantly.

I know he was not trying to play me out. He needed to understand that he was dealing with the major leagues, not the minors. He wanted to roll around here flossing, sending flowers acting like he had money and money ain't a thing, well I was the one to check just how deep those pockets were. All of a sudden you mention The Manor and he tries to come up with all these excuses. I don't leave room for excuses. If he was going to be a baller he betta be willing to play on a full court or either he'd be watching my game from the sidelines. Bam!

"I took the liberty of making reservations earlier, Mr. Booker. I hope you don't mind," I said thinking, 'here we go', but before I could finish my thought, he said, "Of course not. That was gracious of you. As soon as you're ready, so am I."

I thought he would come up with some smooth excuse to go

somewhere else less expensive, but he didn't. I was shocked. He didn't say 'let me make a few calls', knowing he had to run to a MAC machine to get some more money or anything. He didn't even stutter. *'Thank You Jesus. I feel my help coming on.'*

"Okay, Mr. Booker, I will be right out, and thanks again for the flowers," I said as prepared to hang up the phone. Sometimes I make my own self sick. Why in God's name did I have to thank him *again* for the flowers? Lord, I guess the man thought I never received flowers before by the way I was acting. He replied right away, "Kiyah, don't even mention it, I was just so elated that they met with your approval. I'll be waiting."

We hung up and as soon as we did Benita started right in. "Ooooh girl, what's up? Flowers *and* he's already waiting outside. You're blushing all over yourself. Tell him to come in so we can see how he looks."

I couldn't believe her nosiness. She really has a serious problem. A demonic spirit had just taken over all of her dignity and decorum. "Hold it right there, Benita. You're just like Kraft Macaroni. It's the cheesiest and you're the nosiest. I'm not telling that man to come inside so I can make a spectacle out of him just for you to see," I said as I grabbed my purse.

"You need to call up the Elders of the church right now so they can bind those spirits in you before they *completely* overtake you. I'm not lying. You got a nosey spirit in you and it is not of God." The entire office just exploded in laughter, while Benita was sitting there with the dumbest look on her face. I just knew she wasn't serious about me asking that man to come inside so she could see. Then again, yes she was.

"Benita, girl you gotta problem. When I'm on my way back, I will call the office and ask for my messages. That will be my code to let you know that we will be pulling up in five minutes. You can run to the door and see him when he gets out to open the car door for me okay."

Okay," Benita said, now satisfied, "hurry up outside. He's waiting for you girl." I grabbed my sweater just in case it was cool in the restaurant.

"Have a good time Kiyah," everyone said as I was leaving out the door. "I will", I smiled. "I will."

Chapter Three

The Date

As I started approaching the door that lead to the outside of the building. I began to feel a little tingling in my stomach. I guess I was a little nervous, okay, very nervous. Once I reached the glass door, I could see him standing outside his shiny new, midnight black S-class Mercedes Benz. The man was looking so good. Oh yes he was! He had on a black velour Enyce sweat suit and black sneakers at first glance. From the distance I was standing, I could not tell what brand they were. Lord, my knees were shaking as I opened the door to exit the building and as I walked towards him, I was just admiring how clean cut and fine this man was. Of course, this only made me more nervous, because I wanted to make a good impression on him. Now I'm thinking maybe I should have worn my Parasuco Jean suit with the rhinestones all over it, or maybe I should have worn my COOGI dress, the one that shows off all of my curves. Now look at me. I'm just meeting this man, I hadn't even gone on the first date yet, and already I was putting my salvation on the line. I really needed to pray and pray hard, because this man was looking crispy good. The devil sure knows how to prepare a trap for you. If this was in fact a trap, then this man was a magnet and I was the biggest piece of metal in town.

Oh God, as I got closer to him, he had the biggest grin on his face. A warm gentle smile. This gave me the impresssion that he was happy to see me and at the same time he liked what he saw. By the way, the sneakers were Jordan's.

Anyway, as I got within touching distance of him, he opened his arms for a hug, which I sank right into. Lord the man smelled so good! He was wearing a cologne called *Full Metal Jacket*. I know he had to be thinking the same way about me because I had showered with *Love Spell* shower gel. Victoria wasn't the only one with a secret. I also lotioned myself down with *Trezor* lotion and dabbed a little *Trezor* perfume behind both of my ears. Getting back to this hug, child, I didn't want to let go because he felt and smelled so good. It had been a long time since I had been in the arms of a man. Once he released me from his warm embrace, he greeted me by saying, "Kiyah, I was excited about this afternoon, and you look beautiful."

As he opened the door for me, I said, "I'm excited too, Mr. Booker, and thank you for the compliment. You don't look too bad yourself," I said with a smile. What was I talking about 'don't look too bad yourself', the man looked good, I mean mmm, mmm, good! Do you hear me? As he went around to get into the car, I took a moment to check him out. He had a very sexy walk, a very confident stride. He got into the car and immediately asked, "Kiyah, what type of music do you like?"

I answered, "Mr. Booker I like all types of music; gospel, jazz, contemporary jazz, but to tell you the truth I'm not really in the mood for music. I'd rather talk, if that's okay with you?"

Mr. Booker looked over at me with a very satisfied look on his face and said, "That's amazing Kiyah, you know I was thinking the same thing. That's already a good sign for us." He set his navigator system and confirmed with me, "the Manor in West Orange, correct?" "Yes," I answered. He started the engine, but who would have known, you couldn't hear so much as a hum in the engine. His car was definitely top of the line, with piped out seats and plush carpet on the floor. Even the floor mats were custom made out of this plush carpet material. There was wood grain all over the front console, doors and the entire steering wheel. As we pulled off, he asked me, "Kiyah, if you don't mind me asking, how old are you?"

"How old do you think I am?"

I looked at him intensely. My whole body jerked all the way around in the car so I would be facing him, letting him know that the whole date could be shattered by his response. Hesitantly he answered, "Kiyah, I never speculated on a specific number, because your beauty is ageless. I'm just curious. But now that you've asked me, you could be anywhere between twenty-five and thirty. Seriously Kiyah it doesn't matter to me how old you are. I was just curious sweetheart."

I needed to end his song and dance so I quickly interjected with, "I'm thirty-two Mr. Booker." There is something electrifying about this man, and he looked so confident when he spoke, like he knew exactly what he wanted to say. He was definitely not searching for words to say. He looked so good when he was talking and his profile was so appealing. I never even thought I could be attracted to an older man. "Kiyah you're beautiful. You must take good care of yourself," he said.

"Thank you, Mr. Booker. I must admit, I don't always eat the way I should because I'm so busy, but I'm trying to do better," I replied.

"You must be doing something right," he said quickly. I liked him, and now I felt more comfortable, but I was thinking that we needed to reserve some of this conversation for the restaurant. So I turned to him and said, "Mr. Booker, you know I've changed my mind, I would like to take you up on that offer for some music, if you have some contemporary jazz that would be fine, or *whatever.*"

"Sure," he replied and turned on his stereo system from the steering wheel of course. Immediately Rachelle Farrell's voice filled the car with the tune *Welcome to My Life,* which just so happened to be the first song on her CD. The words of the song seemed so appropriate for this point and time. Rachelle sang *"There was a time when I stayed at home alone. I knew a lot of guys, but none that I could call my own. Then you came along and my heart sang a brand new song, now I'm happy, glad I found you and I'm not afraid to say, welcome to my life, come on in and make yourself at home. Welcome to my life."* Rachelle Farrell was one of my favorite jazz artists and I loved every song on that particular CD. The words of the song and Rachelle's distinctive range took me into another zone for a few minutes. I got lost in the music and the atmosphere. This seemed like a brand new world for me. This guy was so classy. Suddenly, he turned and looked at me with the warmest smile and said, "Kiyah are you okay? Is this music okay?"

It was perfect and I was feeling real good.

"Yes, Mr. Booker I'm fine. I'm just enjoying the scenery and the soothing music," I said in a relaxed and satisfied tone, because I was. I was relaxed, comfortable, satisfied and the scenery just took my breath away. The scenery was *him. 'Lord I've got to repent now, for what I might do later.'* It was

48

wonderful, as we rode up the highway. I was just laid back looking straight ahead out the front windshield enjoying the music and the smooth ride. Every so often I could see him out of the corner of my eye looking over at me with a content look on his face.

As we neared the restaurant, he turned the music down, looked over at me and asked, "Kiyah, when can I see you again?" Uh oh, Tonto is back on his horse again.

Shocked, I answered, "I will let you know."

He shot back, "Why can't we decide together?"

Quickly I said, "Let's make it through lunch first and then we can take it from there. Is that okay?"

Mr. Booker was quiet while we pulled up to the valet. Then before the attendant could open the door, he turned to me and said, "That'll be fine, but I can just tell right now that I'm going to want to see you again. I like you. There is something about you. It's special and I can feel it."

"Thank you," I said. I was ready to go into the restaurant. But I felt like he wanted a definite answer first. Boy this felt awkward. "When would you like to see me again Mr. Booker and what do you have in mind?" I said impatiently.

He replied without delay, "Tonight, how about dinner? I know it sounds like I'm too anxious and I am, but I don't want this day to end. I really would like to spend the whole day with you. I feel so comfortable with you Kiyah."

I was thinking 'WOW', spending the whole day with him never even crossed my mind. I was just anticipating making it through lunch and going back to the office to gossip for the rest of the afternoon. "I don't know Mr. Booker, I need to make arrangements, I have children."

Before I could finish, he answered, "You get the sitter and I'll pay for it."

"I couldn't let you do that, I don't know you," I said very softly.

"Kiyah, I insist. Here's a hundred dollars. Call a sitter and let's seal the deal," Mr. Booker said, forcing a crispy one hundred dollar bill into my hand. I thought, he's a lawyer alright. 'Let's seal the deal' sounds like a lawyer to me. This man was feeling me something terrible or he was just willing to go the distance, thinking he was going to get a little action that night. And if he did assume that, he was definitely betting on the wrong horse. 'Cause wasn't nothing happening, ya heard me. Now the hundred dollars did motivate me a little bit. I reached for my phone to call Jamillah, a very close friend of the family, who usually watched my kids for me. I knew I could definitely trust her and feel at ease leaving my kids in her care. Furthermore she only charged me twenty-five dollars. I did the math. It was a seventy-five dollar profit. When I finished my call to Jamillah, I said, "Okay Mr. Booker, everything is set, but really, you don't have to pay for the sitter. I couldn't let you do that." Of course this wasn't really my sentiment, but it was the right thing to say. What would I do if he said okay and took his money back? I would be literally sick. But just as I thought, being the classy man that he was, Mr. Booker replied, "Of course I could. Please Kiyah it's the least I could do." My antennas immediately went up. *The least he could do?* Hmm, that's a thought. He then gestured for the valet attendant to open the door. As I began to get out the car, the valet attendant extended his hand to help me. I felt like the queen that I was. Quite naturally after the other valet attendant opened the door for him as well, instead of waiting for me to come around the car, he walked around to meet me, and as he did, he grabbed my hand to lead me into the restaurant. This place looked more like a huge palace. I was the Queen and maybe, just maybe I'd found my King. I was feeling this; the atmosphere, his presentation, and the attention. It fit my lifestyle, it fit my demands. It was scary to even conceive that I could meet someone that could remotely make me feel like I would even want to dabble in a relationship again so soon.

As we approached the restaurant, the hostess greeted us. She was a well-dressed, tall and elegant woman, appearing to be in her mid fifties. She could be easily mistaken for owning this joint instead of being the hired help. "Good afternoon, welcome to the Manor. Do you have reservations?" she asked.

Mr. Booker answered, "Yes we do. Booker. Party of two."

She looked down at her book and said, "Yes of course Mr. Booker, right this way. Your table is already prepared. We certainly hope everything meets with your approval. If you need anything at all, just have your waiter to get me. My name is Martha Dyer."

As we approached the table, I noticed a huge bouquet of peach roses on the table. I immediately scanned the room to see if this was customary. I didn't see roses on anyone else's table. As I turned my attention back to our table and before I could open my mouth, Martha Dyer said, "The gentleman thought that you would appreciate the smell of fresh roses while dining with us today Mrs. Booker. I hope you enjoy them."

I was stunned at that point, as the waiter pulled out my chair for me to be seated. I said to Mr. Booker, "Thank you. This is so sweet of you. You really didn't have to do this. You've already done enough. I don't know what to say except thank you. They're beautiful." He gave me the sexiest smile I'd ever seen and said, "You can say Leon. Please call me Leon. Mr. Booker seems so formal, like we're strangers. Besides, Ms. Dyer has already made you my wife, 'Mrs. Booker'," he said, and we both started laughing.

I replied "Okay Leon, thank you for this beautiful bouquet of flowers."

He smiled, "Now that's more like it." Suddenly, his cell phone rang and he answered, "Hello." He paused for a moment.

"Yes Bishop." He paused again. "We're hoping to get Madison Square Garden. *Yes... yes...okay.* Everybody's share is one hundred thousand dollars each." Just as his conversation was getting good, my cell phone rang. It was my Dad's house.

I answered, "Hello." It was my nephew Wynell, who's more like a brother because he was raised by my parents. Besides, he's only six years younger than me. He's my middle brother Shotgun's son. Shotgun had Wynell when he was fourteen years old. Brenda was Shotgun's girlfriend at the time. Her parents were so upset that she got pregnant at fourteen. Back then it was unheard of. Now it's as common as catching a cold. But anyway, her parents were so upset that her father cut off the heat in the house when Wynell came home from the hospital. He was born on January 17th and it was below freezing outside. Of course my brother Shotgun with his bad temper had a fit and wanted to kill Brenda's father and make him turn the heat back on. Instead my mother demanded that he go get Wynell and bring him to our house so she could take care of him. The rest is history. Wynell has been living with us ever since. Once or twice his mother tried to get him to come and live with her. He had a fit. He cried and threw tantrums while staying over her house to where my Dad had to go and get him in the middle of the night. So after so many attempts, his mother just decided that it would be best if he just stayed with us. Wynell refers to his mom and dad as 'Brenda and Shotgun'. He refers to my mother and father as Mom and Dad.

He also refers to all of us, his uncles and aunts, by our first names, as if we are just his brothers and sisters.

Anyway, getting back to the phone call. Wynell was yelling into the phone "Kiyah, I just bought a trailer home. I need to park it in your driveway, until I figure out what I'm going to do with it."

I looked at the phone, wondering if he had lost his mind. He didn't even have his own bedroom, let alone a house and he's buying a trailer home. "What?!" I screamed into the phone. "Wynell I don't want no big ole trailer blocking up my driveway. Why don't you park it at Daddy's house?"

Wynell pleaded, "Because Daddy said the same thing. Come on Kiyah, please? I only paid ten thousand for it. I can easily get forty thousand for it. I just need some place to put it for now."

"No, Wynell," I say as I'm looking across the table at Leon, who's off the phone and looking around impatiently. "Look Wynell, I've got to go. I'm at lunch with someone and I'm being rude. I really got to go. I'll talk to you later."

"Kiyah does that mean I can park the trailer at your house until we talk later." I sighed, "No Wynell, I gotta go." "Kiyah, I'll give you one thousand dollars once I sell it," he said desperately. Well now, this brings about a whole new light on the situation.

"How long Wynell," I said giving in.

"Two weeks," he replied anxiously. I was ready to get off the phone and get back to my very handsome lunch date so I consented to letting Wynell park the darn trailer at my house, but of course I couldn't give in that easily. I had to put my foot down. "No longer than two weeks Wynell, because after that I *will* have it towed off of my property."

Wynell, now satisfied, said, "Okay, Kiyah it's already there and the keys are in your mail box. I have two people coming over to see it tonight. I know you don't mind showing it to them, since your gonna be right there."

"Wynell, you know what…!"

He quickly said, "Kiyah, I love you. Thanks. Gotta go." Then he hung up the phone. I had a few choice words for that little bum. The nerve of him to take the liberty of assuming that he could just leave his junk in my yard without my permission. Ooooh, I just wanted to snap, crackle and POP all over the phone. But there was no way I could let Leon see me come out of character. Not yet anyway. So I just had to sit here, grit my teeth and swallow it. I looked over at Leon and he smiled at me.

"Leon I'm sorry, I hope you don't think I'm rude. That was my brother."

"Of course not Kiyah. It's okay. I know how family can be."

His phone rang *again*. He answered, "Hello. Yes, I need you to fax a letter of request over to my office." He paused.

55

"That's the only way I do business. I need everything in writing."
He paused again. "Thank you. Someone from my office will be in
touch with you."

He hung up the phone and started to apologize, but before
he could say a word my phone rang. It was my daughter. "Hello,"
I said.

"Mom, where are you? I called your office and you
weren't there. Where are you?" My daughter was ranting into the
phone sounding like she was almost out of breath.

"I'm out to lunch. Is something wrong? Are you okay?"

"Mom, I'm okay. I just wanted permission to go to the
Boys and Girls Club after school with my friends."

"With what friends Kyasia?" I asked.

"Ashley and Brittney. Mommy please." She knew I
couldn't resist when she put it that way. I was always giving her a
chance to prove she was responsible, but if she blew it, that was it.

"Okay, Kyasia, you can go. I'll pick you up at 6 o'clock."
I told her.

"Mom, why so early?, it doesn't close until 8 o'clock, and
Ashley and Brittany will be staying until 7:30 p.m." Now she's
pushing it. "Kyasia, I will be picking you up at six, I have an
appointment tonight."

"Okay, Mom, thanks I love you, I'll be outside at six."

"I love you too, Kyasia, but don't wait outside, I'll come in
and get you, I'll see you at six." I'm thinking I need to go inside

and see just what kind of kids are hanging out in there. After I hung up the phone, I noticed that Leon had received another call. Okay, enough is enough. I looked at him very intensely and said, "Break that up, this is not working, I need your undivided attention."

Ooops... I let a little bit of "Prince Street Projects" sneak up out of me. He then pointed to my cell phone. I immediately said, "I'm turning *my phone* off."

And I did. Then he said to the person on the phone, "Listen Bishop, I am sitting across the table from a very beautiful woman, and I need to give her my undivided attention, so I will give you a call later, is that alright?" I'm blushing now. He continues, "Okay Bishop, I'll talk to you later." Then he turns to me and says, "Okay Kiyah, I'm going to turn my phone off, but I must tell you I've never been in the company of a woman who is in just as much of a demand as I am."

"Well Leon, I'm not in demand, I just have a very large family and we are very close. However, although I'm not in demand, Mr. Booker, I would like to demand a little bit of your attention right now for polite conversation," I said in my most sensual voice.

Leon replied, "Kiyah, let me make this crystal clear. Not for one moment did you lose my attention; conversation maybe, but not my attention. I haven't been able to take my eyes off of you since you have been in my presence today."

"Leon, you really know how to make a woman feel special, and this is very nice, I'm already enjoying myself and lunch hasn't even been served yet," I said, changing the tone of the conversation, it was getting a little to intense, you know, hot and heavy Lord help me, I'm still a Christian.

"Kiyah, are you ready to eat."

I thought to myself, 'Of course I'm ready to eat, we've been sitting here for twenty minutes. I didn't eat breakfast this morning, so what does he think, that this voluptuous size 12 runs on water?' "Well, yes I was quite famished, I skipped breakfast this morning."

"No problem, sweetheart." He said and nodded his head toward someone behind me. Being the curious person that I was I turned around to see just who he was motioning towards. There was a waiter standing there with two silver platters with silver tops covering them.

The waiter walked towards us and placed the dish in front of me saying, "Madame." And as he addressed me he removed the top of the platter to reveal jumbo shrimp cocktail. My favorite! The waiter continued "Madame, is this satisfactory, or would you be needing anything else to assist your appetizer this afternoon?"

"No thank you, this is fine." He then removed the top from Leon's platter. Now I'm thinking, no this man didn't have this waiter standing in the wings while we were conversating, waiting for his approval to approach our table. I'm also thinking, he had already arranged and ordered our appetizers. The waiter turned to Leon and smiled as he revealed a platter of King Crab Legs. He placed some sort of bib around Leon's neck and then handed him the tools he would use to eat his crab legs with.

Looking quite pleased with the service he was receiving, Leon then spoke to the waiter. "Everything is okay, but please bring the lady a glass of water with lemon and some freshly squeezed lemonade with her main course. I will have the same in that order please."

The waiter quickly replied, "Yes sir," and hurried along toward the prep area. This was too much. Did this man sleep in my house, because he knew me to a 'T'? He must have studied my personal resume. But hold it, I just met this man. How could he be so sure and so accurate? I always order water with lemon as well as lemonade with my main course. How did he know?

I had to ask, "Leon, how did you know that I prefer water with lemon with my appetizer and lemonade with my main course?"

He swallowed the food in his mouth, wiped his lips with the napkin that was resting on his lap and then replied, "I'm sorry Kiyah, I just assumed after our conversation about you bettering your eating habits, that you would appreciate my consideration for your efforts. Let me call the waiter back so that you can order what ever you want sweetheart."

"No, I'm fine. You just seem to know a lot about me," I said. "I'm just amazed that you knew that, but I guess it was just good observation. This is great. Just perfect," I said wanting to reassure him.

He responded with, "That's what you are, Kiyah, just perfect."

Lunch was wonderful. We had shrimp scampi over linguini and a very pleasant conversation. On the way back to the church we just listened to Rachelle Farrell. He reached for my hand and we held each other's hands in silence the entire ride back to my office. We both were feeling something magical. So magical that I forgot to call Benita with the code for her to come and get a glimpse of Leon. Well, too late for that, because by the time I remembered, we were already turning the corner that my church was on. Leon then said, "Kiyah this has been the most pleasant afternoon I've had in a long time. Thank you for your conversation on the way back."

"What conversation?" I had to ask, "we didn't say a word on the way back Leon." I continued curiously.

He smirked and replied, "No we didn't Kiyah, we didn't say one word, but the silence was priceless. It was symbolic of the peace and contentment that we both felt from a very enjoyable and satisfying afternoon. Kiyah, our thoughts were connecting and communicating in a way that our lips would never be able to formulate into words. You feel me?" he asked.

Of course I felt him, "Yes, I know exactly what you mean, because I felt something magical and it was just dancing around in the silence." I agreed. "There was definitely a connection." Leon said looking deeply into my eyes and for a moment we just looked into each other eyes. I broke the tension by saying "Well Leon, thank you so much. I should be getting back to work. I really had a great time."

Anxiously he said "Kiyah, will I be seeing you for dinner tonight?"

"Sure you can pick me up here at seven o'clock."

Leon quickly replied, "That will be fine. I will see you then. Any ideas of where you would like to eat?"

I thought for a minute and then replied, "No Leon. Why don't you choose, after all I did decide on lunch?"

With a raised eyebrow and a very amused look on his face he answered, "You got it, I'm going to make this a night you will never forget!" This guy was something else. He was a little extra though, but hey, I better not complain, my ex was on the opposite end of this scenario. At least this guy was putting in extra work trying to impress me and digging into his own pockets. Now, Michael, Mr. Man, he knew how to plan a spectacular evening, at my expense. I never forgot those evenings. I can't forget them. How can I? I'm still, to this day, paying for them. If I could ever get past paying the interest on those darn credit cards, I might one day get to the actual charges.

First there was Michael, now Leon. I started to pray, because Leon was a breath of fresh air. *'Father, I know I asked You for a saved man, but salvation is for sinners. Is that not right? So Lord can You save him? This would fit right into my description of the man we discussed earlier Lord. You know, the one that wouldn't rebuke me for the way I dress and he wouldn't be no stiff ole deacon. Lord, in the name of Jesus I know that there is nothing to hard for You. God, You said in Your Word that it is your desire, that ALL should be saved. You see there God, that ALL means Leon, too! And that ALL would come to repentance...'*

My prayer was broken when Leon asked me, "Kiyah, are you okay?" Gosh, I didn't realize that I had gone into a trance just that fast. It all was too good to be true. After I came out of the presence of God and back into Leon's Mercedes, I responded by saying, "Yes, I'm fine Leon. Thanks for lunch and I will see you at seven," He helped me out of the car, and afterwards I gave him a hug, which I just wanted to sink right into cause the man smelled *so good.* But you know I had to keep him guessing, so I gave him a curt little hug and proceeded to walk the 'runway' of the sidewalk that led to the church's door. As I was walking away, I could feel him staring at me, but purposely I did not turn around. I continued to strut into the building. As I exited the runway, I turned around to close the glass door to the building, which normally closed on its own. But of course this fit into the part of my performance that would allow me to innocently catch him looking at me. Uh, oh, here we go, I'm turning around and closing the door. Oh my God! He was still standing right there where I left him! It seemed as if he was enraptured with my every move. I guess I still had it. Certain things in life you just never loose. I'm no Vanessa Williams or Halle Berry, but I was blessed with the charisma of life and a heart of gold. I consider myself, and have been told, that I am a very attractive woman. But you know what makes you more attractive? You become more attractive by having a good heart, a positive outlook on life, by carrying yourself with respect and honor and if you allow the love of God to shine through you, there is no limit to your beauty. As a child, I always envied my friends, because to me they were much prettier. I stilled loved them and appreciated their friendship and I never treated them mean because they were liked by what I considered the more 'popular' boys in school.

My dad was strict, so I could not, as Daddy would, say *take company* anyway. Then to make matters worse, I got a bad perm by Ms. Fanny, who had been the beautician in our family for years and all of my long beautiful hair came out. This happened at a very crucial time in my life. I was just turning twelve, had braces on my teeth and to put icing on the cake I had fractured my right wrist playing tag football in the street. So here I was going into the eighth grade at the height of puberty with a cast on my right arm, metal going all across my grill and my hair was a total mess. After Ms. Fanny's fiasco my hair wasn't even long enough for me to even put it into a ponytail and my mom didn't want to press and curl it because she didn't want to damage it any further. So all I could do was brush it back with grease and water and tie it town. But of course as the day progressed in school it would slowly lift itself out of place, and by the time school was ready to let out I looked a total hot mess. Can you picture it? I can't stand to even think about it.

The Lord sure had me in mind when He sent those Koreans over here with a product for anything you might be lacking. Hair, nails, pedicures, lashes, glue, wigs, cheap but good make-up, lip gloss, fake jewelry and fried chicken wings for a dollar fifty. Child, ain't no reason for anybody to look bad now a days or hungry either. Those Koreans will sell you the tip of a chicken wing if that's all you can afford and won't allow you to be a penny short on your bill, but will always be hollering for a tip when they deliver food. I don't give tips, because the tip is that I'm patronizing their business. It's a service they provide to deliver the food to my door. But enough about those Koreans, let's get back to me.

Anyway, by the time I went to high school, my hair had grown back in, my braces were off, I now had a beautiful smile, and my cast was history. I started getting a lot of attention from the 'elite' crowd. I was being asked out by the captain of the basketball team. I had tried out and made the varsity cheerleading squad. Heeeey, that little bald-headed, knobby-kneed, Tom-boy had blossomed into an attractive young lady. Although they tagged me as a church girl and knew I wasn't the fast type, guys still called on me and came over to sit and watch movies with me under my Dad's supervision of course. It was my observation that these guys had to like me an awful lot to put up with the third degree that my five older brothers would give them, and the fact that I wasn't loose and afforded as much freedom as most of my friends made it worse. The only time I was able to be around boys outside of our home was when I was at cheerleading practice that was at least three days a week. This happened to be at the same time and place the basketball team practiced. See my point? I, at that time never thought I was really pretty, but just really nice. I still don't consider myself really pretty, yet with a little help from my Asian connection, (you know those Koreans) a girl can bring some noise to the streets. It's not what you do; it's how you do it. It's not what you have; but what you do with it. It's not how you look; but how you present yourself. The most unattractive man can be well-dressed, clean cut and smelling good, and he would undoubtably be so appealing to me. I hope you get my point, because I truly need to move on.

Anyway, as I helped the glass door to the church offices to close, I saw Leon looking dazed in my direction. I gave him a little good-bye wave and started walking down the steps. I opened the bolt lock door, which led directly inside the building, and once inside I gathered myself together. This was more than even *I* expected, and I just want to enjoy this moment for a few seconds before going inside the office to be bombarded with questions and stares and all of the phony mess. Sometimes I just want to be real, just be totally real with myself, no sarcastic responses, no pretentious gestures, nobody trying to impress the other person. Sometimes I get tired of all that. I know that God sees all and you can't hide anything from him, so maybe that's why whatever is in me comes out. It may not be the right thing to say at times and maybe it might be a little uncalled for when I just let someone have it, but that's me, that's how I am, and because people now a days have issues and I am not the one.

I gathered myself together and walked down the hall and around the corner, which lead to the main corridor to my office. Benita caught a glimpse of me and she started running towards me. It was not a pretty site.

"Kiyah, you back? Why didn't you call with the code?" Can you believe this? I guess the elders didn't rebuke that demon out of her yet. "Benita, I'm sorry. I forgot. We were so caught up in conversation that I totally lost sight of our plan. But anyway, trust me, you will get a chance to see him. I'm sure I will be seeing more of Leon." Benita replied rather suspiciously, "Leon? That's his name, Kiyah Leon Booker, that name sure sounds familiar."

Then my curiosity rised. "Benita do you know him?"

"Not off the top of my head Kiyah, but his name sounds really familiar. Anyway, you had a great time, so you will be seeing him again. Did he ask you out again already?" She asked with the enthusiasm of a cheerleader.

"Yes he did. We're going out to dinner tonight." Benita's whole face lit up

"What time, I hope before five thirty, because that's when I get off. I know he's picking you up from here, 'cause I know you ain't stupid enough to have some ole man you just met come to your house already." Benita is a mess; she could care less about a man coming to my house. She just wanted to make sure he was coming to the office so she would have a chance to see him.

"Of course not Benita. You know perfectly well, one lunch date or three for that matter does not qualify any man to have the privilege of being invited to my house, where I live with my children. Anyway, Benita he's not picking me up until seven. I guess you will just have to wait until our next lunch date."

Benita stood there for a moment in deep thought and then said, "Wait my foot, I have some paperwork I can finish and some filing I've been meaning to get to for some time. I *will* be here." Benita is a trip to the circus. She is too funny. I finally entered my office and made my way over to the desk. No messages were on the phone. Something was wrong. This was highly unusual. Even when I was at work all day I had voicemails, from calls I missed due to heavy call volume or something. The phones weren't even ringing. There was no clamoring and talking. What was going on? Had the Rapture taken place? As I turned around in panic to see if anybody else was left behind, I swerved my chair around only to find the entire office staff standing in the doorway staring at me. That was a sigh of relief, 'cause Lord I thought I had been left behind. But then again, the sight of these so-called Christians didn't give me that much more reassurrance, cause they ain't no saints either.

Anyway, Pam, our receptionist, was the first one to speak. "We're not allowing you to leave this office until you tell us everything that happened at lunch today. I have retrieved all of your messages and have determined that none of them require your immediate attention. Furthermore, I left a voice message on your system stating that you will be out of the office for the day and should be contacted tomorrow unless it is urgent. Otherwise, they may dial zero and speak with me for further assistance. So what's up? Can a girl get the scoop?" Wow, maybe Pam needed to be promoted to administrative staff! It's amazing how gossip can motivate people to unimaginable strengths.

"Okay, guys come on in and sit down," I gave in. After an hour of going over the day's events *and* leaving a great deal out (they didn't need to know everything, just enough to amuse them), everybody seemed happy. They grilled me hard, but I was a trooper. I didn't reveal an ounce of the intimate details. But I noticed when I announced Mr. Booker as Leon, Sandy's eyes got really big. I guess I couldn't help but notice because I was still peed off from earlier when she answered the phone in the office and announced that his voice sounded familiar to her.

Anyway, I was exhausted. "Pam, that was a lot of ingenuity on your part. It was sooo brilliant. Now I need you to carry out your strategic plan for the rest of the afternoon, because I'm leaving for real and I will see you guys tomorrow. Thanks a lot Pam. Smooches to everyone. Have a good day," I said as I gathered up my things and sashayed out of the office. I gave them a performance everyday. They lived for it. Pam's face was perched. She was just fit to be tied. I know she didn't think for one minute that she could pull that diva move off on me in an effort to get some gossip and not think that the master of divas, *which is me*, would not get the final bow. She wanted her gossip, so I gave it to her.

As I exited the runway in my one and only true diva style, I proceeded to let Pam have it. In one star-studded motion I gathered up my bags, swung my weave over my shoulders, then threw on my Jackie O' look alike shades and proceeded to leave the office, not once looking back, and knowing full well that she was just standing there with her mouth wide open. She had gotten it (*told off*) by a true diva and she could not come back from it. See every now and then I must let these young girls know the difference between the teacher and the student. I didn't mean no harm, really I didn't. But I just couldn't resist letting her have it.

She had been begging me for it for quite some time now. I was annoyed by all of her stares and the way she was always checking me out from head to toe everyday when I came into the office. Furthermore, helping herself to my personal messages and voicemails. Oh yes! Girlfriend invited herself to that party and I inevitably had to crash it for her.

Now that she had caused me to use unnecessary energy, I had to find a way to get the kids, get home, feed them, go over homework, brief Jamillah on what I expected her to do while watching my kids, then finally take a few minutes to unwind, take a nice long candlelight bath with my Sweet Temptation bath gel from Vicky's Secrets. I had to then give myself a quick facial, and find something to wear all in four hours. Well, I knew I could do all of the above in less than two hours, except for finding the right thing to wear tonight. On second thought, maybe I needed to just order a pizza to give myself more time.

I went straight to my house to just check everything out. I had to pick up a few things we might have left hanging around while rushing out this morning and just quickly go over the bathroom. I'm very particular when it comes to my house. It is always presentably clean, but when I know I'm having a guest over I like for things to be immaculate.

Once I finished straightening up the house, I realized it was time to pick the kids up from school. I could for once take my time since I happened to be in the area, when usually I had to leave from the church, which was at least twenty minutes away. After picking the kids up from school, I headed towards Jamillah's house, which was off highway 280 in Newark. My cell phone rang and for some reason, before even looking at the caller ID, I knew in my spirit who it was. I felt it. It was Leon, and as I looked at my phone while it was ringing, sure enough it was his number. Knowing it was him I cleared my throat and took my voice up one octave and said, "Hello."

His voice came right back with "Hello sweetheart, this is Leon. How's everything going?"

With a silly grade school girl grin I replied, "Everything is going great Leon. I anticipate being on time for our dinner date tonight, that is, if you're still taking me out."

"Of course Kiyah, I'd be a fool to pass up any opportunity to be in your company."

I've never heard that one before. There was something that was awfully intriguing about this man. He spoke with such authority, sort of like a professional speaker. I made a mental note to ask him his profession at dinner tonight. "Okay Leon, I have my kids with me and I don't feel comfortable talking to you in their presence so I will see you tonight. I hope you understand."

He replied with a pleasant tone, "Absolutely, in fact I respect that Kiyah, really I do. That says a lot about your character, and I look forward to seeing you at seven tonight. I have a few surprises for you. See you then."

Quickly I replied, "Okay, I will see you later. Good-bye."
By the time I hung up with him I was in front of Jamillah's house
blowing the horn. Jamillah came right out of her house, hopped in
the car and we were at my house in ten minutes.

Chapter Four

Prelude to Dinner

It was six o'clock and I was totally relaxed and at peace. I had the whole house to myself. Jamillah had taken the children to the park after they finished their homework to give me some quiet time. I was soaking in a Victoria Secret's Sweet Temptation bubble bath with a dozen floral-scented candles surrounding the tub. As I was soaking, I contemplated what to wear and began having second thoughts. Maybe I shouldn't have accepted his invitation for dinner so quickly. I should have made him wait. Things were moving too fast, my head was spinning. My heart was telling me that he wanted to see me as bad as I wanted to see him, so I put my mind on a time-out and surrendered to the atmosphere. I gave myself a cucumber facial and another twenty minutes in the tub. It felt so good laying there in the warm bath, just chillin, maxin and relaxin in total peace. When I got out, I heard my cell phone ringing and prayed it wasn't Leon. I told him that I would see him at seven and I hope the brother doesn't turn out to be pushy. Unless, of course, he is pushing those big faces (money) my way. When I answered it, I wished I hadn't, because it was Michael calling. What in the hell did he want? "Hello" I said, annoyed. Then the voice of death spoke. "Hey, Kiyah what's going on?"

I was thinking, 'Hey, my foot. Aint nothing going on but CHILD SUPPORT.'

"Listen, Michael I'm very busy. If you wanted to speak with the children they're not home right now, but I will have them call you when they get in." I don't know but it was only the grace of God that allowed me to be courteous to this poor excuse of a man.

"As a matter of fact, I didn't call to speak with the children. I wanted to talk to you. Kiyah I'm doing bad and things are not working out for me and my girlfriend." Good for him, but why in God's name was he telling me? I noticed the time.

"Michael I'm sorry to hear that", but I was really thinking, 'Good for the BASTARD.' "But I really need to go. I guess you won't be sending the money you promised this week. That's cool, send it when you can." Which would probably be never. He had only sent four weekly payments in the last six months. I needed to end the conversation. "I really have to go now, I don't want to be late. Ooops!, I mean, I need to get back to the movie I was watching. It's about to go off." Why was I lying to protect his feelings. He didn't care about my feelings when he was parading around town in the car I was paying for with his little tramp.

He got amped and screamed, "WHAT DO YOU MEAN YOU DON'T WANT TO BE LATE KIYAH? LATE FOR WHAT?!" I knew I didn't have to answer to him. I should have hung up the phone. On second thought, though, I waited six months for the opportunity to clear the air on Michael.

"Michael, at first I wanted to spare your feelings, because I know what it feels like to be in your shoes. But it shouldn't be painful for you at all Michael, because I don't have to answer or inform you of my comings and goings anymore. More importantly, it's none of your business but since you asked, I don't want to be late for my date tonight. Yes Michael, I have a date with a very nice man." Then I went in for the kill. "And Michael this is not the first date. The kids will be fine. Jamillah's staying over to watch them. I'm sorry to hear about your problems, *really* I am, but I really gotta..."

He interrupted me by yelling into the phone even louder this time. "YOU WHORE! YOU'RE LEAVING MY CHILDREN HOME WITH SOMEONE ELSE SO THAT YOU CAN GO SLUTTING AROUND?!" Before he could finish his tantrum, I hung up the phone. It was now six-thirty and I was pressed for time. I rushed upstairs and got dressed. Thank God I had envisioned what I wanted to wear while soaking in the tub. I put on some black slacks and a black netted sort of see through blouse with a black camousal underneath. Then I slipped on my black strappy sandals which were trimmed with rhinestones. The final touches to this outfit would be the custom-made rhinestone belt which fitted loosely around my waist; simple but sharp at the same time. I put on my rhinestone watch and earrings. I quickly did my face and was out the door by six forty-five. I didn't get a chance to kiss the kids good night because they were not back yet. I planned to call back home around eight to make sure they had gotten back from the park and to say good night. Within minutes, I was pulling up to the church.

By the time I pulled up to the church, Leon was already there sitting in his ride. I was happy to see him because I wanted him to check the ride I was cruising in. Benita was there too, with her face plastered to the door of the church. Curiosity got the best of homegirl because she had the expression of pure shock on her face. But I had no time for Benita now. I needed to check the full package my date for the evening was wrapped in. As I was preparing myself to get out of my car, Leon hopped out of his car, looking like a double dip of butter pecan ice cream. Child this man looked good, I mean he was so polished. He was wearing an off-white linen short set and camel and off-white diesel sneakers. Nice. Underneath his top, he wore a camel-colored tank top. His golden colored legs looked so appealing in this gear and his muscular build was totally in order. He opened the door for me and said, "Hello, sweetheart are you all set."

I gave him the biggest hug once I got out of my car. "Yes, Leon I'm ready to go." We held hands as we walked towards his car and when I got in I noticed a package in the backseat. I wanted to turn around to see exactly what it was so bad, but I didn't want to appear to be nosey.

"Are you ready for a night you won't forget Kiyah?" Leon asked once he was in the car and started the engine. I laughed and told him, "Yes I am. Put it on me Daddy,"

"Watch out now. "Kiyah I like your style and before we go anywhere let me express how beautiful you look this evening, why don't we just fly to Las Vegas and get married." Okay, Tonto has entered the building once again. I knew he hadn't just said what I thought he said.

"Leon, what are you talking about we just met. Calm down sweetheart let's take things nice and slow,"

"Kiyah I don't want to scare you, but I am a man that is used to getting what he wants and not to sound arrogant, but I'm a very intelligent person and I have this keen sense of judgement when it comes to people. I can tell right now that you're the one. When I first saw you at the restaurant and the way you carried yourself, I knew right then and there that there was something remarkably special about you. You're gifted, special, intelligent, beautiful, confident and I want you to be mine."

Well now, he sure does have good judgement when it comes to people because he had me sized up to a tee. "Leon, thank you. I feel awfully flattered and I feel the same way about you, but let's just see what happens. I don't know if I told you, but I was married for twelve years and I'm not even divorced yet. I don't want you to get the wrong impression. I have no intentions on ever going back to my husband and we are now in the process of getting the divorce. I'm sorry but I'm not ready for anything serious right now. Do you think that we could just enjoy each other's company and let things happen on their own? I was thinking that this date was over before it even got started.

But his next statement made me feel comforted in an instant. "Kiyah, that's okay. A man can try. I see what you don't see sweetheart. But in time you will see it too and if you don't, I'm willing to work hard at changing your mind. Are you ready, because we're here?" What was he talking about? Moments later, we pulled up in front of a huge parking lot with a big garage sitting in the middle of a lot.

"We are where Leon?" I asked puzzled.

"Just a second baby give me a minute," Leon said as he beeped his horn. Within a few minutes, the metal fence rolled back so that he could pull his car into the gate of the parking lot. The garage door opened and a white navigator limousine rolled out. A chauffer got out and opened my door. "Ms. Kiyah will you please come with me." He reached for my hand and I flashed Leon a *WHAT IS GOING ON*! look. He nodded his head to let me know that everything was going to be fine. I looked back to see if Leon was going to come as well. I was thinking that little sneak wanted to get me away from the vehicle while he was trying to hide his package which was probably for some other woman. Here he has only known me for a minute and a half and talking about getting married. It will be a cold day in hell first. Once again, my head was spinning. My mind was racing. After 15 years of marriage I wasn't ready to think about or even deal with marriage. But the limo *was* nice. It had the mirrors on the ceiling, with lights and the crystal glasses were lining the bar that was adjacent to the seats. The experience instantly took my mind off of Leon's agressiveness. I learned the hard way, not to sweat the small stuff. I was just going sit back and enjoy the ride. If you're going to deal with a hustler, be prepared to deal with and accept everything that comes along with it. You know the old saying, *'More Money More Problems?'* It's so true. These guys out here that are hustling and getting all this money, it all looks good, well the money looks good, but what comes along with it will have you *dead on arrival*. The women, the drugs, the cops, the guns and the danger alone is enough to say it ain't worth it. But oh no not us, we don't think that far ahead, instant gratification is what we want. I was thinking, *'Speak Lord. I hear you loud and clear. This ain't nothing but another trap of the enemy. After this date, I'm not seeing Mr. Leon again.'* My thoughts were interrupted when Leon got into the limo and to my surprise he had the package in his hands and once he was inside, he handed it to me and said, "Kiyah, this is for you. I don't know if you noticed it when you got into the car. I didn't want you to see it. I wanted it to be a surprise, but I couldn't fit anything else into the trunk."

I was thinking, 'couldn't fit *anything else* into the trunk'? "No I didn't see it. Where was it? My god Leon, you are just too much. You don't have to do these things sweety, really you don't. Can I open it now?"

Pleased with my excitement he said, "Sure, you can, but why don't you wait until Miles brings all of the things inside first." Was this a dream or what? You know I was all wrong about Leon. Look at me already calling him sweety. That had just slipped out in all of the excitement. Again, the limo door opened and the limo driver, which I assumed from what Leon said was Miles, had a stack of gifts which was so high you could only see half of his face, and all of them were wrapped in silver paper with black and silver ribbons around them just like the one Leon had given to me. He proceeded to place the gifts in the long seat that was to the left of Leon and I. I was overwhelmed at this point, if all of these gifts were for me, and this was an indication of what life would me like with him, then I was willing to reconsider his offer and jet to the airport right now. So what, if it didn't work, at least this time I would be compensated for my tears. I turned to Leon and when I did I noticed that he was just sitting there working on his laptop like it wasn't any big deal to him. "Leon, are all of these for me?"

He didn't even look my way, but lifted his finger and said, "Just wait a few more minutes sweetheart and then you can open your gifts while we're on our way to the show."

Once again the door opened and it was Miles. There were more packages wrapped the same way, and Miles proceeded to put the gifts on the seat and when he had them neatly stacked against the seat and on the floor, he stepped out the vehicle and went on Leon's side opened the door and said to Leon, "That's all sir, it is seven thirty, the show is starting at eight. Should we be on our way?" Leon, looked up from his laptop to respond to Miles. "Yes, Miles, thank you. We can leave now." Miles shut the door and before I knew it the door from my side of the limo was opening and it was Miles again "Ms. Kiyah can I pour you a cup of champagne, wine, or juice before leaving." Stunned I said, "No, Miles, that's quite alright, I can get it myself. Thank you anyway." Miles quickly responded, "You're quite welcome Ms. Kiyah" and shut the door. Within minutes the limo was moving but with the tinted windows and all of these gifts demanding my attention I did not bother to notice what direction we were going in.

Leon's phone rang, but right before that he looked like he was about to say something to me, but instead he answered his phone. "Hello. Yes. Not right now," Leon said into his cell phone."Okay, I will be there. You can talk to my people about the particulars. They will provide you with my fee and rider information." Hmm, rider information, sounded like he's an entertainer, just as I thought. I made a mental note to ask him his profession as soon as the opportunity presented itself, so that I could be sure. Leon continued with his conversation, although he seemed to be somewhat annoyed with the person on the other end. "I understand, however I cannot and will not discuss that information with you. That part of the deal is handled by the people in my office. I hope you understand. I'm sorry, but I'm in the middle of a very important meeting and I have to go. Thank you for your interest and someone will be able to help you at the office in the morning. They're normally there at nine sharp. God bless you." He's an entertainer I thought *and* he believes in God, or maybe he was just being polite. Now I'm wondering, I mean seriously wondering what does this man do, one things for sure he is *very* important.

My curiousity was getting the best of me, so I decided to ask Leon his profession. "Leon, sweetheart" and as I did he stopped me.

"Kiyah sweetheart, I'm sorry I will be right with you and I promise you will have my attention for the rest of the evening. I just need to handle one more thing."

At first I was like, I know he is not trying to cut me off, WHO IN THE HELL does he think he's talking to? But since he put it that way I just said, "Okay, sure Leon, that's fine." He picked up his cell phone and started dialing, while he was waiting for them to answer he closed his laptop and proceeded to put it in the leather carrying case sitting next to him.

The person must have answered, but what came next I never expected "Paul, why are people calling me on my cell phone for engagements? I don't appreciate that. Why should I pay you people if I have to deal with these people anyway. You find out who in the office is giving my cell phone number out and fire them immediately." Leon was speaking with a very angry tone and his forehead was all frowned up. He continued, "Paul, I don't want to hear that, look I need my time for studying and for preparation. I don't need this, do you understand? Handle it. As a matter of fact, I'm going to have my number changed in the morning." It seemed as if this argument was going to linger on for quite sometime. Then Leon looked over at me and his anger instantly eased, his frown suddenly softened and he spoke in a more subtle tone. "Paul, I'm due in Dallas on Friday and I need you to make sure my suits are cleaned and my things are packed. I'll be coming straight from Teaneck to the airport and I won't have time to go past the house. I'm depending on you to make sure everything is taken care of. Okay Paul, I've gotta go. I'm out with the young lady we saw at John's yesterday. Paul, man she is the one," he continued while smiling at me. "I'm sure she's going to love everything. Listen, I've gotta go. I will let you know." Leon was off the phone and I was trying to make out the other side of his conversation in my mind. I wondered which one of the other two guys Leon was with yesterday at John's, was Paul.

Anyway my thoughts were interrupted when Leon spoke to me. "Kiyah, I'm sorry you had to hear all of that, but I needed to handle that while it was fresh on my mind." I like a man with authority, firm when it comes to business and as sweet as a teddy bear when it comes to dealing with a lady.

"Leon that is fine, don't worry about it, I understand. By the way Leon what is it that you do for a living?"

He smiled and said, "What do you think Ms. Kiyah?" Now he wanted to play games. He ain't Fifty Cents and this wasn't twenty-one questions.

"I shouldn't have to *think* Leon, when I can just ask you and get an answer." He showed an expression on his face, like he was impressed by the way I answered him, but his game continued. "Kiyah, I'm not going to tell you what I do, I'm going to show you. I'm going to be in Newark on Thursday and I want you to come down to Living Well Baptist Church at seven o'clock. Do you think you can make it?"

Thursday's I had to take Kyasia to dance school and pick her up and anyway I didn't feel like playing these little kiddie games. "Leon, Thursday isn't good for me, so why don't you just tell me now?" What is the problem? Why wouldn't he just tell me what he does? It was getting ridiculous. "Then you will just have to wait. I want it to be a surprise. I normally don't reveal to people what I do so soon, but there is something about you, I feel like I can trust you." What is all this I feel like I can trust you stuff? Was he a secret agent or spy or something? I didn't have time for this. "If your job is dangerous or risky, let me know right now, I don't want to put myself in any danger," I said rather annoyed.

"Kiyah, sweetheart, it isn't anything like that, not at all, I just have to protect myself and what I have." You know what, this was really getting on my nerves and after Michael I only had a few nerves left.

"Leon, why is it so difficult to just tell me what you do? Why does it have to be an issue? It's a simple question. Definitely an appropriate topic for first date conversation. What is the problem?"

Leon moved closer to me now and put his arm around my shoulders to calm me down. He was very amused by all of this and then he said, "Okay, Kiyah please don't get upset. I assure you that you will understand in the long run why I was hesitant to tell you what I do. Just trust me. Why don't you open up your gifts now. We should be at our destination soon and I want you to relax." Now his arms around my shoulders immediately sent chills down my spine. This man was extremely charismatic. It was just unreal and he smelled so good. You can just tell that he wore very expensive cologne.

"Leon, are all of these for me?"

He then looked into my eyes with a sly grin on his face seemingly satisfied by the excitement I was displaying, and responded, "Yes, Kiyah all of these gifts are for you sweetheart. Why don't you start with this one," he said as he handed me the gift from the backseat of his car. This was really exciting. I mean it was like a dream. Nothing like this had ever happened to me before.

As I was taking the gift out of his hand and placing it on my lap getting it into position to unwrap the very elegant wrapping paper, I turned to Leon and said, "Leon, this is awfully sweet of you, but you don't have to do all of this. Leon, I don't want you to think that you have to always buy me something or give me something. I want the foundation of this relationship to be supported by friendship, trust, honor and respect. I really need you to understand that."

Leon looked at me with a hint of disbelief in his eyes and then he smiled with that magical smile of his and said, "Kiyah, you know you have been able to do what no other woman has ever been able to do before."

I interjected immediately by saying, "and what is that?"

He came right back with, "You impress me. You're sincere, smart, beautiful and what amazes me the most is the fact that you're really *believable*." I just looked at him. I was speechless. At that point we were looking into each other eyes so intensely and sitting extremely close. I felt like I wanted to kiss him but before I could contemplate on the kiss, he leaned in and kissed me and when he did, I mean the moment his lips touched mine I was at Tinkerbell's palace in Disney World. This kiss seemed like it lasted an eternity, but as his fingers started rolling down my back I felt my plane landing and I was back in the limo.

"Leon, I don't want things to move too fast," I said prying myself from his embrace.

At the same time Leon wiped his forehead and adjusted his shirt and said, "I'm sorry Kiyah, it was an impulsive move on my part, I apologize. Now why don't we start opening up your gifts or else we won't have time. No more talking young lady, let's get to opening these gifts." I smiled and started opening the package that he had handed me and once I tore off the wrapping paper I could tell right away that it was an electronic device from the type of box it was in.

I was able to read it and it was a verizon cellular phone. I turned to Leon in disbelief, "Leon, honey why did you get me a cell phone? I already have one. I know we discussed my bad reception and everything, but you buying me a cell phone, I assumed you were just joking."

Leon looked at me and smiled, "Kiyah, when I say I'm going to do something, I'm going to do just that. It's already on, all you have to do is charge it for a few hours before using it, when you turn it on, it will display your new phone number; I already have it locked in my phone and sweetheart I never joke when it comes to my lady."

Here we go again Leon had that look in his eyes and I could feel another one of those kissing moments coming on, but all that mushy stuff was going to have to wait, I had gifts to open. I immediately broke the ice.

"Leon, thank you, but everybody at work and all of my family already have my old number. What's the point of two cell phones? I'm not that important."

He quickly said, "It's for me Kiyah, so that I will be able to reach you when ever I want and you will know that when that phone rings it's me or one of my people. Besides Kiyah, you are, as you can see very important to me"

"Okay Leon I'll keep the phone, you are something else." I opened the rest of my gifts during our ride and they consisted of perfume, a foot massager, two scented candles, a box of Godiva chocolates, a beautiful chain with a crucifix on it from Tiffany's and several boxes of Lingerie from Victoria Secrets (now what was he hinting at?). As I was thanking Leon for all of the wonderful gifts, I noticed that the limo had stopped, before I knew it, Miles was opening the door. Instantly I could tell that we were in New York City. We were in front of a theater and the Marquis read BRING IN THE NOISE/BRING IN THE FUNK starring Savion Glover. I was really excited! I love Savion Glover and I had been wanting to see this show for some time now. How did he know?

The show was awesome and Savion was really great. The performances were spectacular. But after leaving the theater, I thought we might be heading back home when I saw the limo heading towards the Hudson Parkway. But to my surprise we were going to the port and Leon had arranged for a cruise around the Hudson. We talked and looked out at the ocean and the beautiful city lights. The cruise was very romantic and there was entertainment. Everything was surreal. There were a few moments while on the top deck that we just hugged and kissed and caressed each other. We decided not to eat on the boat because Leon had made reservations for B. Smith's on the Roof Top. Dinner was also wonderful and the atmosphere in B. Smith's was just breathtaking. There was a live band playing on the roof top and behind them were all window, from the floor to the ceiling.

It had started to rain by the time we were seated which was probably about eleven o'clock in the evening. The room was dark with only candles providing the light at each table. It was an awesome atmosphere with the rain running down the windows and the band playing. It was absolutely the most romantic experience I've ever had. The food was excellent. I had steak, rice and vegetables and Leon had salmon and vegetables. After eating, Leon pulled his chair close to mine and we cuddled while listening to the band.

Before you knew it, it was past midnight, I needed to get home, I did have to work tomorrow. Leon called for Miles to meet us in front of the restaurant. Then he called for our waitress to bring him the check. After taking care of the bill he escorted me downstairs and out of the restaurant where Miles was already waiting. Once in the car Leon turned to me and asked, "Kiyah did you enjoy yourself tonight?" As if he needed to ask. Couldn't he tell by the Howdy Doody sunshine girl grin plastered on my face.

"Oh my God, yes Leon, I must say that this was one of the most enjoyable evenings that I have ever had and thank you so much I enjoyed myself immensely," I said.

"Kiyah how many siblings do you have? I remember your two sisters from lunch earlier today. I was just wandering if there were more."

"I have five brothers and just two sisters, the two you saw today."

"Really, you have a big family, it's just three of us. Two males and I have one sister. I couldn't imagine growing up in a house with that many siblings. That had to be very hard on your parents. What does your dad do for a living?"

"My father is the Pastor and founder of the church that you picked me up from today. My mother before she passed was the assistant pastor." I paused and then continued, "They did a great work together and I'm sure that they had some rough times along the way, but God has been merciful, he has done a great work through my parents."

Leon sat up in his seat and he seemed very intrigued "So you're a PK? That's awesome. You know they say that we are the worst." What did he mean WE? I know he wasn't a preachers kid, but then again he could be, because for real we are the worst. It seems like the devil will work on us harder than anybody else. I know my parents had been through a lot with us while trying to do a work for the Lord. My second oldest brother Vincent was shot five times right in front of our house, while my parents were at church on a weeknight. He lived, but he was paralyzed from the waist down. My brother Shot Gun has spent most of his life in jail for various different types of criminal behavior. My brother Jerome who is only two years older than me was slipped bad drugs when he was fifteen by a neighborhood friend, which as a result caused his mind to go bad. But the sad part about it, he was a genuis. He was the valedictorian of his eigth grade class. He was awarded the honor of being mayor for a day. It was very heart breaking because he had an extreme amount of potential. My brother Tony, who is four years older than me had our home raided for drugs and everyone knew my parents pastored a church. This *had* to be extremely embarassing for my parents. But they stood right by us, no matter how difficult the situation was. See, the devil was using their children to hinder their progression in the ministry. But they remained faithful to the calling on their lives and God allowed them to be like Job. No matter what was going on at home my father would make it to church and preach the Word of God with power and anointing. My dad never missed a Sunday at his church in twenty seven years; he has remained faithful to the work he is doing for the Lord. I respect my father because he loves to teach people about the Lord our God. Anyway I was listening to Leon and he was just so amazed that we were both preacher's kids and we had that in common. "Kiyah, I knew there was something special about you."

"By the way Leon, what do you do for a living? I know you didn't think that you were going to get away without telling me."

He sat back in his seat. "Oh come on Kiyah, you will find out soon enough, I have to go to Dallas on Friday, it's a business trip, but I can find time to entertain you, if you would accompany me?"

"Whoa slow down Leon I don't want you to get the wrong impression. I am not ready for that type of relationship." I'm a little pissed off now. He was thinking that since he bought a sista dinner, took her on a boat, to one of the hottest shows on Broadway and lavished her with all of these wonderful gifts, that he is automatically entitled to some hanky panky. I guess normally it would have definitely qualified him. But not with Kiyah. I was still saved, sanctified and I don't get down like that. Just cause he had strayed away from the church and lost the presence of the Lord didn't mean that all PK's had, so he might as well get that thought out of his mind.

"Kiyah, I'm not saying that you have to be ready for anything, I just want your company and nothing more." He paused looking at me for an answer and then said, "I promise." I had never been to Dallas and the kids would be with their father. Why not? It wasn't costing me a dime.

"I don't know Leon, it sounds great, but I will need my own room and I don't know if I can prepare myself that fast. It's already Tuesday, no it's actually Wednesday (it was already after midnight). I just don't know." He then put on that smile that things were working out the way that he wanted them to. "Kiyah please, I invited you. You're traveling with THE MAN! You don't have to prepare a thing. Just show up at the airport and I will get you everything you need once we arrive in Dallas." This was definitely my kind of man, Cause you know what I was getting sick and tired of all of these guys out here trying to get a free ride. The game has definitely switched instead of women looking for men who have a good job; men are out here looking for women who have a good job, to take care of them. They have no shame in accepting money from women nowadays. Instead of being shamed, they are proud. They think they're the man when they walk around all day doing nothing and chillin with their boys while their woman is at work making ends meet to pay the bills. I will NEVER apply for that position again. I don't even want to conversate with a man who doesn't have a job. Leon was a breath of fresh air. It was good to see that men like him still exist. But the majority of the men these days are a mess. It just seems as if the saggier the pants got the more their values and morals went down. The bigger the t-shirts got, the bigger their egos got. Even the ugliest, fattest, nastiest guys with no car or job or hustle will try to play you nowadays. "Leon you know what, I think I might be able to go with you, only if you promise to get me my own room."

"Kiyah, it's a deal." We talked a little while longer and as we were approaching the Lincoln Tunnel, Leon pulled me under his arm and held me. We just listened to the soothing music and before you knew it, I had snuggled up under his arm and fell asleep on his chest. When Leon tapped me to wake me up, we were in front of the church. "Kiyah sweetheart, we're back."

"Oh okay," I said while wiping my eyes and trying to get myself together. I hoped I hadn't snored or slobbered on this man. I was so tired, I had fell into a deep sleep. Leon walked me to my car and I gave him a big hug and he waited until I started my car before he went back to the limo. Miles then waited until I pulled off before he proceeded to leave. Chivalry was not dead. This was truly a great evening. I spent an entire day with this man and he didn't get on my nerves not one time. I was impressed. When I got home Jamillah was asleep on the couch, with the phone in her hand. I didn't bother waking her. I eased the phone out of her hand and put it on the charger; put some cover on her and went upstairs to take a quick shower and get into bed. I was really exhausted. To my surprise, I went to sleep like a baby for the second night in a row.

I woke up Wednesday morning at seven-thirty, I didn't even here the alarm when it went off at six-thirty. Thank God, Jamillah had gotten the kids up and dressed and fed them. I had to rush out the door with sweats on, in order to get them to school on time. Everytime I looked over at Jamillah she just kept smirking at me. Kyaisia kept asking "Mom, what's wrong with you, why you couldn't get up this morning? Where did you go last night?"

"Kyaisia, I was just a little too tired this morning that's all, and I told you last night that I was going out with a friend." Finally I was pulling up in front of her school and thank God because she was really digging into me with the questions. "Okay Kyaisia have a good day in school. Here's your lunch money. Love you."

"Love you too Mom," Kyaisia said as she got out of the car to meet up with her friends as she headed into the school.

Kaseem wasn't saying a word in the backseat of the car, this wasn't like him. So while I was turning onto the block that his school is on I asked, "What's the matter Kaseem?"

"Nuthin Mom."

"Kaseem, honey why are you so quiet?."

"Because you went out last night and didn't take me."

"But Kaseem, you couldn't come with me. Where I went they don't allow children. Besides, you don't need to be out on a school night."

"But Mom, school will be over in two more days, it's not like I couldn't miss. Besides Kyaisia was trying to boss me around."

"I'm sorry Kaseem. I will have a talk with her."

His face lit up. "Mom are you going to spank her; that's what she needs. She was acting like she was my mother or somethin'. Ask Jamillah."

I looked over at Jamillah and she was cracking up. "Okay Kaseem, I'm going to get Kyaisia, I assure you it won't happen again. Here's your lunch money and you have a good day in school okay sweety. I love you."

He was happy now and back to himself and he hopped out the car and said, "I love you Mom" and ran on off to play with his friends until the bell rang for them to get in line to enter the building. Jamillah turned to me and said "Ms. Kiyah, Kyaisia wasn't bossing him around she was just making sure he didn't do any of the things that you won't normally allow him to do."

What did she just say? "I don't understand Jamillah."

"Oh, I mean that Kaseem was asking me to do certain things like, he wanted to ride his skateboard in the house and Kyaisia was like, "No, my mother doesn't allow him to do that. Those sort of things, it was no big deal but Kaseem was really mad at Kyaisia." I got what she was saying. "Oh really. That boy is a trip. He is so sneaky. Look Jamillah do you want me to drop you

96

off now or can you wait until I change for work and I can just drop you off on my way to work?."

"No problem Ms. Kiyah. I can wait for you to change."

"Thanks Jamillah. You are the best. Here's your money and a little bit extra for this morning."

"No, Ms. Kiyah you don't have to pay me any extra. I don't mind at all."

"I know Jamillah, but I want to. I really appreciate your help." Within minutes I was home, Jamillah went straight in and started cleaning up from breakfast. I went directly upstairs to get dressed. I was already running late for work, so I had to rush. After dropping Jamillah off at home, I got to work at nine-thirty. I was only a half-hour late.

I was only in my office for ten minutes, when I could tell that there was a different vibe in there today. At first I thought it was my fatigue and I was just imagining things. But ten minutes had went by without Benita running off at her mouth with some gossip. Pam was unusually quiet and there wasn't a lot of laughter and giggling going on. Anyway I wasn't in the mood for it no how. But still it seemed very strange. I didn't chase it though, I didn't ask anyone any questions or anything like that. Benita kept looking at me and shaking her head like I had done something wrong. She really wanted me to ask her what her problem was, but I was not going to give Ms. Girl the satisfaction. Whatever was eating away at her today, let her swallow it. I couldn't be bothered

. I was tired and moody, and my co-workers did not want to catch it from me this particular day. God being the Good God He is, has chosen that day for all of them to be talking underneath their breaths and not so much as trying to hold a *brief* conversation with me. Good, cause I was not in the mood. Around three o'clock Leon called me on my private phone and we made small talk. I had the kids in the car so I limited my conversation. He wanted to make sure that I was still going to Dallas and he assured me that he had reserved me, my own room. I dropped the kids off at Queen Bee's and headed back to the office. Suddenly I was in a good mood. When I got back to the office everyone was talking and laughing and back to normal. But the moment they noticed my presence, they went back to that same behavior from the morning. Something was up, but you know what, they were so phony in the office and so jealous, it didn't even botha me. I knew Benita with her big, wide mouth had told them about Leon. Instead of them being happy for me, they were mad and jealous, because they didn't have a man pursuing them like that. Well if they only knew, that I envied their situations as well. Most of them had their happy homes and husbands who loved them. I'll admit, this wasn't the way I wanted my life to turn out. At thirty-two I didn't want to still be in search of a partner or companion. I should have been celebrating my thirteenth wedding anniversary. But I was not going to put up with their phoniness for another minute. "Sandy I'm leaving for the rest of the day and I won't be in for the rest of the week. I'm going to use some of my sick days. I will clear it with Queen Bee."

Sandy had this smirk on her face that just made me want to say, 'and what is your problem Ms. Sandy?' But I didn't.

"Kiyah is something wrong? Are you not feeling well?" Sandy asked in a laughing way.

"I feel fine Sandy. I have time and I want to use it. I don't need to explain or inform you of the specifics," I said rather annoyed that she could be laughing at the same time that she was inquiring about me being ill or something.

"Excuse me, Kiyah you don't have to get smart, I was just being concerned," Sandy said while moving her neck from side to side.

"No, Sandy you weren't being concerned, you were being nosey." Sandy jumped up from the desk and she was looking like she wanted to go pound for pound with me.

"You know what Kiyah, you are always getting smart with people and I'm tired of your mouth." This is what I wanted. I needed a reason. "You're tired Sandy and I am just as tired of you as you are of me, with your sneaky ways; always trying to get into my business. Asking people where they're calling from, and if they are related to somebody else you know by their last name. You think you're running a game, but I have already folded your hand a long time ago girlfriend. Everyday you gather every bit of information from here you can and before the sun goes down it's already down at Jesus is the Answer Church on Springfield and Washington St."

Benita jumped up in between us trying to calm us down. Sandy was yelling at the top of her lungs by now. "No Benita get off of me, cause I am tired of her. She thinks just cause her father owns this church and her sister owns this business that she can just talk to people any way she wants to. Move Benita, I'm going to whoop her behind." Just what I needed. I wanted and had prayed for this day. "Bring it on Sandy, I'm not scared of you. I'm saved, but I'm about to back slide and ask for forgiveness later. Move Benita. Move and stay out of this."

Benita was standing in between us "Kiyah I'm not going to let ya'll fight, don't disrespect yourself like this, don't disrespect the house of God like this." Benita had a point. I shouldn't be doing this. I had to get a hold of myself. "Sandy bring your behind outside!" I said and started outside. Benita threw her hands up and let Sandy go. Once I was outside I took off my heels, walked further down the street away from the church. I was ready for her. I was tired of people thinking that just because I'm the Pastor's daughter that they could just say or do anything to me and I had to take it because I'm the Pastor's child and I can't make my parents look bad. This was my chance to finally get some of that frustration out. As Sandy was running out the building towards me, everyone in the office was in tow. You know those cows aint gonna miss a good fight. As Sandy was coming towards me like a bull, I was bracing myself and getting ready to go at her. She must have gotten within ten feet of me when I heard someone calling me in the other direction, when I turned back around Sandy was trying to run up on me and sneak me, but right before she could do that Ever Ready jumped out her car and punched the daylights out of Sandy. It looked like Ever Ready had three fist. Later everyone declared it was only one punch. She knocked Sandy clear off her feet. It happened so fast I was mad. I wanted the satisfaction of letting her know once and for all that she was NOT the one. Once everything had registered, I noticed that Ever Ready had left her car in the middle of the street with the driver's side door still open. "Ever Ready! Why didn't you let me get her?" I said defiantly.

"Kiyah, shut up! You betta be lucky I came when I did. She was about to sneak you from the back."

"You betta pull your car out of the street and come inside cause we're going to have to explain this to Daddy and Queen Bee," I said while gesturing to everyone to go back inside.

By this time Sandy had gotten up and was still talking smack. "They jumped me, they jumped me, Kiyah couldn't fight me one on one." Was this grade school or what?

"You know what Sandy I suggest that you leave and come back and meet with Queen Bee tomorrow. Cause you don't want no more parts of Ever-Ready today." At first she looked like she still wanted to get all hyper, but then she noticed Ever Ready had parked her car and was heading back towards us and she said,

"Yeah, I think I'm going to leave and somebody is going to pay for this assault. I hope your daddy does have a lot of money, cause he's going to need it," she said as she was walking away.

"What you say Sandy?" Ever Ready hollered as she started running towards Sandy to get her again. Sandy took off running, in fact she never went back inside to get her things. Ever Ready and I laughed for awhile with Benita as she wanted detail by detail of everything that happened down the street. Once we satisfied Benita's appetite for gossip, we left and went up to Queen Bee's to break the news of what we had done! I really thought that she was going to be so upset, that she was going to have a heart attack. Instead she was relieved. Number one she was glad it happened off of church grounds. Second she said that Sandy came down the street wanting and looking for a fight. Third, Sandy never saw Ever Ready hit her, she never saw it coming. Fourth and most importantly she would be back tomorrow begging for her job because she started so much mess everywhere she went, nobody else would hire her. "I'll have Fredricka draw up a new contract for Sandy that she must sign in order to keep her job and it will include clauses that will enable her to sue the business or the church," Queen Bee said calmly "Now Kiyah what is this I hear about you using some sick days and not working the rest of the week?" she said in a very *I am sick of you* tone.

I explained to Queen Bee about Leon and how everyone in the office was acting. Once I told Queen Bee about last night, the

102

gifts, the limo and all of that. She was like. 'Get HIM Girl!' We all just laughed. It was good being with my sisters. We are very close and they mean a lot to me even though I don't tell them that. But I'm sure they know. Queen Bee she can resolve any situation and smoothly I might add.

The next day she woke me up at ten o'clock "Kiyah, guess who's at the office asking for a meeting with me? Queen Bee said in a voice that was just a little above a whisper. "Who? Sandy" I guessed.

"Yes, I told you. Do I know my stuff or what?" Queen Bee replied. I've got to admit she is good, I hope to one day be like her.

"Girl you are good, but why are you whispering?" I questioned "Cause Kiyah, she is waiting outside my office, I just wanted to call you and Ever Ready first and let you both know what was going on. Go by Henry's and get your nails and toes done it's on me. We've got to snag Mr. Leon, girl your sista is on the case, and Kiyah, get your eyebrows arched and your upper lip and chin waxed. Your big sister is going to show you how to do it. With this type of man you have to be DONE from head to toe. Okay I've gotta go, Call me when you come from Henry's we've gotta go SHOPPING. I've got to get you ready for Dallas. He's getting you your own room, right Kiyah?" What would I do with out my sister? I don't want to ever find out "Yes, Queen of course, what were you thinking, I got excited by all of his money and just lost my salvation? Besides, you know me better than that," I said then she made one last comment before hanging up. "Alright, because you know the Simmons' women don't play that. I've gotta go. Get your butt on up and get to Henry's. We've got work to do." With that she said good-bye.

I got up, got dressed, went to Henry's got my nails and toes done. Then I had my eyebrows arched, then my chin and upper lip waxed. Boy, did that hurt. Just as Queen Bee said Sandy needed her job and was more than willing to sign the new contract to maintain her position. Later, Queen Bee and I went to Short Hills mall. She bought me everything from dresses to pant suits to pajamas to luggage (Fendi luggage I might add) and shoes. By the time we got finished shopping it was eight-thirty in the evening and by tradition we went to Johnny Rockets to get an old fashioned hamburger and some onion rings for Queen Bee and chili cheese fries for me. Queen Bee was like a trainer, she briefed me on how I should conduct myself on this trip and what to watch out for to determine if there was a significant other in his life. This is normally the type of things all three of us would discuss with our mother if she was here, she would be right here with us letting me know just what to do. Queen Bee is so much like my mother it's amazing. Well, by the time we left the mall it was after nine and I was tired, but anxious and anticipating tomorrow and this trip to Dallas with Leon. Strangely enough I didn't hear from him at all today. However, it was Thursday and he did say that he had to be at Living Well Church for some type of function. I guessed he was busy. After dropping Queen Bee off at home and thanking her for everything, I rushed over and picked Kyaisia up from dance and then picked Kaseem up from my dad's house and headed home. Once we'd arrived at home the kids immediately took their baths and went to bed. I decided to pack my bags and then pack their things to go to their father's house on the next day. Then I took a quick shower and went to sleep.

Chapter Five

Dallas

My excitement this morning caused me to wake up when the sun was making its debut. I was full of anxiety. I went into the kitchen to get a glass of orange juice and I saw a message on the cell phone that Leon had given me.

"Hello Kiyah, this is your man," Leon said and continued. "Look sweetheart, I need you to answer the phone, that's what I bought it for. I'm exhausted and I wanted to be with you tonight, instead of going all the way home."

WHAT DID HE JUST SAY, I said to myself as I looked at the phone, then I continued to listen, "I mean you have to be closer to the airport than I am and we could just leave from your house together. Call me back and let me know."

I deleted Leon's first message and listened to the second message. "Kiyah, why haven't you called me back, you need to understand that my work takes a lot out of me and when I'm finished I need to be with my lady, but I guess you're already sleep so I will see you at the airport in the morning. Our plane leaves at 10:20 A.M. You should arrive two hours prior. We will be flying Continental Airlines, go to the domestic ticket counter and give them your flight time, destination and your name. There will be an e-ticket reserved for you. If you need me to send Miles for you, I can arrange that. Just let me know, if not, I will see you in the morning." Now what was Leon, talking about, 'when he gets finished *working* he needed to be with *his lady*.' He didn't call me until well after midnight. What kind of *work* was he doing?

Okay it was six o'clock and I didn't want to be running close to the time I was supposed to be at the airport. I decided to put all of our things in the car, then I woke the kids up so that we could start getting dressed. By seven-thirty we were on our way out the door. I dropped the kids off at their schools, dropped their bags off at Queen Bee's house so that their father would be able to get them later. I was cruising down highway seventy-eight on my way to the airport. Once I got onto highway one and nine, the airport was within my view. I was getting nervous; this was the first time I had ever done something like this before. As I approached over-night parking, my stomach was feeling queasy. I had a lot of bags and maybe I should have gone up to the departure gate first. But I didn't, because Newark's Airport is so crazy, ever since the nine-eleven attack you can barely stop your car to let someone out, without a police officer motioning for you to move. So I decided to call Leon, as the phone was ringing I started to change my mind, but before I could he answered "Kiyah, what's wrong? It's ten minutes after eight. Where are you?" he said without even saying hello.

"Good morning to you too Leon, I'm here, I'm in overnight parking and I'm wondering how I'm going to manage getting my bags all the way over to the gate."

"Listen, you don't have to worry about that. I'll send Miles for you tell me your location."

"I'm in lot C section 25." Within minutes Miles was pulling up towards me only this time he wasn't dressed up like a chauffer and he wasn't driving the limo. When Miles got out the Blue (Eddie Bauer) Expedition, he looked young, like maybe twenty-five no older than twenty-eight. He had on a throw back sweat suit, baseball cap to match and some fresh sneakers. "What's up Kiyah, are your bags in your trunk?"

Shocked by his demeanor, he was talking all hip and not so elegant and poised like he was the other night. This was two different people. "Mile's is that you?" I asked

"Yeah, oh about the other night, he always has me to do that when he's entertaining a new one," Miles said with a broad grin on his face.

WHAT did he just say. "Mile's I didn't hear you correctly." Miles had a look on his face as if he had just let the cat out of the bag.

"Look Kiyah, I don't want to bite the hand that feeds me but you seem like a nice girl and I'm just saying be careful."

"Careful of what Miles? What do you mean a new one?" Miles cell phone rang, he answered it and all I could hear him say was, "Okay, okay we're on our way now." After he hung up the phone, he spoke very fast "Kiyah open your trunk and let me get your things we have to get you to the gate right away, time is short." I did as he asked. I opened the trunk. He put my things into the jeep he was driving. He opened the front passenger door and helped me into the jeep and we took off. While we were driving I decided to see if I could get some more information out of Miles. "Miles do you think I should even be taking this trip?"

He didn't even look my way. "You know what Kiyah, you're a grown woman and don't pay any attention to what I just said. It's hot outside and I'm just frustrated."

Now wait a minute, something was up and I needed to find out. "Miles you don't have to worry about me telling Leon anything, besides I just met him and I don't want to be traveling to another state with a psychopath or axe-murderer." Miles started laughing, "Kiyah he's none of those things. Look, just see where he's coming from before you let your heart get involved. I've seen several women get their hearts broken." Miles continued, "But you know what Kiyah, you might be the one, you're the first one I've seen that has a little going for yourself on your own. Most women are out to get something from a brother and willing to accept anything to get it. You seem to be different. I want you to enjoy yourself. He's a good man. It's just that a man in his position shouldn't do certain things. It just isn't right." Before I could ask Miles what was his position, he had stopped the jeep and we were in front of the Continental Airline's departure gate. Leon was standing outside with six other guys waiting for me. Miles proceeded to get my things and have them checked. I walked up to Leon and gave him a hug and as I did I looked back at Miles and winked (just to let him know that I wasn't going to act any differently) so that Leon wouldn't suspect that he told me anything. He smiled back and took off in the jeep. Leon walked me inside the airport and over to the ticket counter, after I showed my identification, I got my ticket and within hours we were boarding the plane. Leon and I sat in first class, the other six guys sat in the coach section. I slept most of the flight and Leon was reading and studying on his lap top. When the flight attendant brought our food I woke up and Leon immediately said "Kiyah you haven't said much, is something wrong sweetheart?"

"No, Leon I'm fine. Just a little tired." Leon was suspicious "What were you and Miles talking about when he picked you up from the parking lot?" He *was* guilty of something. "Miles and I were just talking about how difficult it is to get around at the airport especially now while they're doing new construction."

Leon, with his eyebrow raised said, "Kiyah, I know Miles and I hope you're telling the truth. You see, Miles is my cousin and he's always been jealous of me and in my profession you have to be careful of who you let into your inner circle because people will try to bring you down. They want what you have. They're jealous of your capabilities, so they will do and say whatever it takes to destroy you." He paused for a minute and went on. "I don't let just anybody get close to me. I'm careful about the people I have around me. Those guys back there, they travel with me all the time and I can trust them. But Miles, he's upset because I don't allow him to be a part of everything I do. He wants to hang out with me and travel with me, but I know that he can't be trusted. So sometimes he might make up or conjure up his own fantasies and his own imaginary series of events concerning my character. In other words, Kiyah, he knows nothing about me except for driving me from one place to the other and he's only been working with me for five months."

Leon was a very smart man, maybe he was telling the truth. Miles might be upset, because he's not traveling with Leon. I know how the hired help can get a little pissed off when they see you living it up. I've been on both sides of that scenario. "Leon, I understand what you're saying, but Miles was just talking casually, nothing concerning you."

Leon seemed to relax a little. "Okay Kiyah, I just don't want you to listen to other people when it concerns me. Give me a chance to show you who I am before someone else paints a whole different picture." He went on. "People are very jealous of who I am and the ability I possess and they don't want to see me with a beautiful woman such as yourself and I want our relationship to be stronger than that, so let's not keep any secrets."

"Okay Leon," I said as I dabbed at the food that the stewardess had left for me. Before I knew it, the pilot was announcing our arrival in Dallas and it was already ninety-seven degrees there. I was glad I packed some shorts and tank tops. Once we got off the plane and headed downstairs to the baggage claim. Leon pointed out to me that the "fellas" will get our things and meet us at the hotel. So we went past the baggage area where there were a lot of men standing with signs indicating who they were waiting for. Once Leon saw his name on one of the signs he started approaching the man. Immediately the man noticed him and came up to him and said, "Bless you, Welcome to Dallas, Pastor. Let me take your briefcase for you, the car is right outside waiting for you."

PASTOR? Leon was a Pastor? My God I would have never thought! I kept my cool, and acted as if I didn't even hear that. When we got outside there was a black Lincoln Continental waiting for us, the man opened the door for us and we got in. Since the word Pastor, I hadn't said a word. I didn't even blink an eye at Leon. As we rode, the man was talking and pointing out landmarks and different things of interest to us. Leon was being polite, they seemed to be very familiar with each other. I didn't say a word. Once we arrived at the hotel, the man asked us to have a seat while he went to get the room keys. "Pastor, can you provide me with your assistant's name so that I may be able to get her key as well?"

"Sure, my brother, it's Ms. Kiyah Simmons, thank you."

"Great," the man answered and went over to the front desk. This hotel was beautiful, definitely five star. I didn't want to confront Leon right now, it would show a lack of class. I was thinking about the conversations at the restaurant on our first lunch date; how he kept referring to the person on the other end of his phone as "Bishop" and how he was ending conversations with "God bless you" and his "*working*" at Living Well Baptist Church on Thursday night. Okay, this was all coming together for me now. Well, Lord, I guess I asked you for a saved man, *but a PASTOR*. Your Word says that You are able to provide above and beyond what we can ask or think. I know that's right. Lord, I asked you for a saved man, you sent me a Pastor, I felt like praising Him right then, but I put it in reserve until I got into my room. Those people might have thought I had gone crazy if I just broke-out shouting right there. They wouldn't understand. Under my breath I was just blessing the Lord, '*Hallelujah, thank you Jesus*' repititously. God is so Good ALL the time. Leon was just perfect for me. He was distinguished with a thuggish edge. He was smart and successful and he has his own church. I might be able to get used to the idea of being a Pastor's wife. My mother did it for twenty-two years and she was an excellent example of how a first lady should carry herself. A first lady's wardrobe is to die for. Especially if you know how to do it and I don't mind getting lost in training, if you know what I mean.

Before I could finish fantasizing, the gentleman was back. "Okay, Pastor Booker, I have your keys as well as your assistant's, I'm ready to escort you to your rooms." I made a mental note to check Leon on this assistant stuff. But for now I would just hold my peace.

"That's okay, my brother, we are fine from here. Besides, I think we will stop in and have a bite to eat while waiting on my armorbearers. God Bless You."

The man looked a little surprised and said, "Okay, then I'll just give your things to Ms. Simmons and be on my way."

As he tried to hand me Leon's briefcase and jacket, Leon quickly grabbed it from his hand. "I can handle that, my brother. Now tell your Pastor that I will be reaching out to him before service. God Bless You." I just knew he betta had got his own jacket and briefcase. I ain't nobody's assistant. Once the young man walked away Leon turned to me and said, "Are you ready to go upstairs?"

Confused, I replied ,"Yes, but I thought you wanted to get something to eat?"

"No, I just wanted to get rid of him. I know that you are now aware that I am a minister, but with you I can be myself and some people don't understand that. Although I am anointed and filled with the Holy Spirit of the living God, I am still just a man. A man with needs just like any normal man."

"Praise God, I understand Leon, I feel the same way. I want to be able to be myself and I know that I am saved and filled with the precious gift of the Holy Ghost, but I don't want to feel like I can't look good or wear jeans or get my nails done and feel like it's not of God. The Bible says that we are fearfully and wonderfully made and it also says to come as you are. Now don't get me wrong, I know there are certain things that are not appropriate. Like mini skirts, and showing cleavage and wearing tight form-fitting clothes in the house of God. But I'm talking about throwing on a pair of jeans on a Saturday night to go to the movies or painting your toe nails. What I'm trying to say is, I like doing things that make me feel good about myself and I think that as long as I do things in a tactful way, I shouldn't be condemned or preached to about it. People should not judge each other, but let God be the judge. Salvation is a personal thing. But I really understand where you're coming from, Leon."

Leon's face brightened up so much you would have thought the sun was beaming inside the hotel. "Good, Kiyah, I'm glad you understand. I knew that there was something special about you. I think the Lord has finally sent me an angel. Let's go upstairs." So we went upstairs and he let me into my room which was right next door to his. In fact, it had an adjoining door. Leon came in to make sure I was satisfied with my accomodations. Who wouldn't be? The room was beautiful. Leon arranged for me to have a fruit basket and fresh roses in my room. Before he left to go to his room he said, "It's now two o'clock in the afternoon, why don't you get some rest, I need to get some as well before addressing God's people on this evening. When you wake-up, Paul will take you whereever you want to go. Here's my credit card. Get what ever you need and here's some cash just in case. I will drop in to see you when I get back from preaching tonight."

"But, Leon, I want to come and hear you speak tonight."

He smiled and said, "I'm not ready for that yet, Kiyah. Why don't you just relax, okay."

"Leon, I want to see, how the Lord uses you. Let me come tonight please?"

He looked a lot more serious now. "No, Kiyah, not now, I don't want to expose you to my colleagues just yet, give me a little more time. You know as a pastor, people will always be talking and taking things the wrong way. Although you and I know that there's nothing ungodly going on between us, people will jump to conclusions. So for now, until I formally announce our relationship, we have to do things discreetly okay, sweetheart, I'm sorry."

Well, I can certainly understand where he was coming from because church people will talk. "Alright, Leon, I understand," I said. "And I certainly understand your perspective and how church folk can talk. So I don't want to do anything that will compromise your integrity. You said I can get anything I need or want." I wrapped my arms around him and gave him a very sensual hug.

"Humm, Kiyah, you smell so good, you can get anything you want. Let me take a look at you," Leon said as he twirled me around to get a look at me. I have to admit I was sharp. I had on some beige cargo capri's with drawstrings at the bottom and a linen short sleeve shirt to match, beige high heel sandles that tied all the way up my leg and my hair was done in an upsweep but a little wild at the top, on purpose. After sizing me up Leon said, "As a matter of fact here's another credit card. Girl, you make a man wanna spend all his money." Leon looked at me like I was a hot buttered buttermilk biscuit. We were laughing and just having a good time talking when Paul knocked on the door with my luggage. After Paul left, Leon followed him. I had a feeling they had some things they wanted to talk about. Leon was so fine and I didn't have to even check him on this assistant madness cause he fully explained himself. I guess as a young Pastor, he had to keep his personal life private. I unpacked a few things, hopped in and out of the shower, put on one of the silk gowns Queen Bee bought for me, laid across the King sized bed and drifted off to sleep.

The phone rang and woke me up. It was now six forty-five in the evening. I answered the phone hoping it was Leon, but it was Paul. "Praise the Lord, Sis. Kiyah… This is Brotha Paul. Did I wake you up?"

"Yes, Paul, but that's okay, is something wrong?"

"No, I just thought that you would like to go to the mall or something and I didn't want it to get too late for you."

Very good thinking on Paul's part. "Thanks, Paul, as a matter of fact I would like to go looking around, you don't mind?"

Paul laughed and said, "Of course not, Sista Kiyah, it would be my pleasure to escort such a beautiful woman of God around for the evening."

"Paul, you're too much. Give me fifteen minutes. Where should I meet you?"

"No need to meet me, Sista. I'll be at your room in fifteen minutes. Wear some flats, the mall is huge."

Fifteen minutes is not enough time for me to get myself together, but I had to try. I threw on some khaki shorts and a white tank top and stepped into some white high heel mules. I wrapped a chiffon scarf around my head like a gypsie and let my hair fall down past my shoulders to give my look a little flavor. Paul and two of the other men were at my door in fifteen minutes flat. "I'll be right there," I yelled as they were knocking on the door. I grabbed the credit cards and cash, put it in my Gucci bag and proceeded to walk out of the room. "Hi, Paul. I'm sorry I didn't get your names," I said as I turned to the other two gentlemen who were standing there with Paul."

They smiled. "God Bless You, I'm Mike," the first one said while shaking my hand.

"God Bless, I'm Brotha Thomas, good meeting you, sista, are you all set to go." Mike was a reserved sort of cool guy, but Brotha Tee, I can tell that he was a hum dinga in the streets before God saved him, because he was smooth from the door.

"Yes, I am, I'm ready when you are." Just like that we were off. It wasn't until we made it to the front of the hotel that I realized that Mike and Tee were riding in a separate car from Paul and myself. Both vehicles were black Lincoln Continentals. Once inside the car I turned to Paul and said, "Paul, are Mike and Tee accompanying us to the mall?"

He smiled. "Yes, Sista Kiyah, that doesn't make you feel uncomfortable does it?"

"Of course not, Paul, I don't want to inconvenience anyone, I know you guys want to be at the service on this evening to hear Leon speak."

Paul's grin widened even more. "Sista Kiyah, don't worry we will make it to the arena long before Pastor takes to the podium, besides, he sent Mike and Tee along to help carry your packages."

Seems like Leon anticipated me doing a whole lot of shopping, so now I can't let him down. "Okay, I guess everything is settled then."

We were at the mall within fifteen minutes, and it was indeed huge, just as Paul had said. The first store we stopped in was Gucci, *my favorite*, where I bought a bag for myself and a wallet for Leon. After that it was Charles Jourdan for shoes and then Armani, Fendi, Christian Dior and Louis Vuitton. On the way out I couldn't resist a vest out of Donna Karan that was made out pure cow hide, trimmed in lamb skin. The guys didn't seem to mind at all escorting me around this huge mall for two hours. In fact, they seemed almost accustomed to it. They just took my bags with a grin and followed me to the next stop. It was now quarter after nine and over five thousand dollars later, I figured it was time to go. "Paul, is this the exit that's near the car?"

He looked at me and said, "Yes, it is. Are you sure you're ready to go? Please don't feel rushed on our account, the mall doesn't close for another forty five minutes." He said it with such a warm smile on his face. I see why Leon chose these men to travel with him, they had treated me like a queen and they were very poised and polite.

"I'm really ready to go, Paul, unless you guys have some things you need to get."

They all laughed, then Mike said, "Only women have to shop in every city they go to." After we left the mall, we were back at the hotel in record breaking time. Paul asked me if I needed anything else once we arrived at my room.

"No, Paul, let me open the door so that you can put the bags inside." And that's just what they did. After they left I decided to order some room service. I was hungry. Shopping has a way of doing that to you. Thirty minutes later my food was delivered. I ate, took a shower, and fell asleep across the bed with just my towel on. It must have been two o'clock in the morning when Leon was tapping me on my back. Startled, I jumped up. "Leon, you scared me."

He was laughing. "I didn't mean to scare you, sweetheart, I just wanted to see you." Leon was looking at me almost in a trance.

"What's wrong, how was service?"

Leon didn't say a word at first, then I realized that I was sitting there with just a towel wrapped around me. "Uuh, nothing's wrong, Kiyah, you just look so beautiful. Uuh show me what you got from the mall."

"Okay, but let me put something on first."

Leon wiped his forehead. "Yeah, you do that, I'm going to get out of these clothes as well. I'll be right back." Once I came out of the bathroom with my pajamas on I noticed it was after two in the morning. I started gathering my packages out of the closet to show Leon the wonderful things I had purchased today. While I was bending down Leon must have came up from behind. He put his arms completely around my waist as to help me get up. "Kiyah," he said while holding me close to his body from behind. His voice was like a whisper and the man smelled like fresh morning dew. Help me, God! "Kiyah, I preached the house down and the people were slain in the spirit. *I* blessed them like never before. I'm still high from the anointing that *I* sent through that place." He was still holding me from behind, while whispering in my ear. "Kiyah I need you. When you're anointed like I was, it leaves you with a desire, a yearning, an appetite that can only be satisfied with…"

I turned around and put my finger on his mouth to stop him from finishing his statement. "Leon, I am so glad that God used you the way He did and that through you He blessed his people. But, sweetheart, I am not your wife and although I want you, I can't be intimate with you. The Bible says that it's better to marry than to burn."

Leon looked very annoyed, in fact, he stopped holding me and was pacing the floor. "Listen, Kiyah, don't preach to me. DO YOU KNOW WHO I AM?"

No I didn't know who he was, but I know who Jesus is. Now I was getting upset because he had raised his voice at me, once he detected that he wasn't going to get any nooky-nooky. Well too bad. "Leon, I'm sorry, I don't want to upset you, but I'm not that type of woman, so if this is what you expect you can return all of these things and put me on the next thing smoking back to

Newark," I said while pulling out my suitcase and preparing to pack.

Leon stopped pacing and his face softened. "Kiyah, I'm sorry," he said while grabbing my suitcase and putting it back in the closet. "Kiyah," he said while grabbing my shoulders and turning me around to face him. "Sweetheart, I'm sorry, I'm really sorry. I don't know what came over me. I never felt this way about a woman before. I'm overwhelmed by your inner and outer beauty. The connection I felt with you from the beginning has me in awe of what can follow. I apologize for my behavior. I just want to be near you and smell you. Please, Kiyah, can I just lay down with you and hold you until we fall asleep. No hanky panky, just hold you, okay. I promise I'll be good."

I was so glad he had found his senses, cause it would have took an act of God, for me to surrender that red Gucci bag. "Okay, Leon, there's nothing wrong with holding each other. Do you still want to see the things I purchased today or what?"

He sat on the bed and I stood over him. He grabbed my hands and looked deeply into my eyes. "How much did you spend?"

I was nervous not knowing what to expect. Did I spend too much and was he going to be upset when I told him? "About five thousand, I hope that's not too much, because if it is we can certainly return whatever you want."

Leon didn't say a word, his expression didn't even change. He just kept looking into my eyes. I broke the ice by grabbing the Gucci bag and pulling out the box that contained the wallet I had bought for him.

"Leon, this is for you." I handed it to him, but instead of grabbing the wallet, he grabbed my hands and pulled me onto the bed, kissing me and caressing me. My flesh was getting so weak. Lord, you know it has been a long time.

"Leon, I can't." As though he had not heard a word I was saying, Leon was undressing me.

"Kiyah, you are so beautiful, please sweetheart, I need you." I tried to pull my pajama pants up but Leon, pulled them off completely.

"Leon, I can't do this, I'm sorry. I'm saved, I can't."

Leon looked at me, for a split second I thought he was mad but then he smiled at me. "Kiyah, listen baby. I want to marry you and I am going to do that right now. Would that make you feel better?"

What was he talking about now? 'News flash Tonto; I'm not even completely divorced yet.' "Leon there's no way we could marry right now, besides we just met. I don't even know you that well."

Leon raised his hand in frustration. "Oh, so you don't know me that well? Well you know me well enough to spend over five thousand dollars of my money in two hours flat. You know me well enough to know that I can take care of you and your two kids. You know me well enough to know that I can put you in a lifestyle that you could not have imagined in your wildest dreams." He stopped for a second, with such an amused look on his face. Then he continued, "Now, listen Kiyah I told you when we first met that it doesn't take me more than three dates with a woman to determine whether or not I want to be committed to her. Didn't I?"

In shock, I answered, "Yes."

As he paced the floor, he said, "First of all there are a thousand young ladies that would die to have the opportunity I'm proposing to you. You're blessed and you don't even realize it. Don't block your blessings, Kiyah. Secondly, there is nowhere in the Bible that indicates you have to get a license or any such thing to be married. So there's nothing stopping us. Thirdly, the Bible also declares that if a man commits adultery against his wife, she is freed from the marriage and is able to marry again. Are you following me, Kiyah?"

"Yes."

"Now, did your husband cheat on you?"

"Yes." If I didn't know any better, I would have swore that Leon was preaching to a congregation.

"So you are Biblically able to become my wife. I don't live by what man says. Kiyah, I live by the WORD OF GOD. You see, man says one thing, but my Bible tells me another. Who you gonna believe, Kiyah, man or God?"

125

I was so stunned I didn't say a word. "Who you gonna believe, Kiyah? I know you're gonna believe the Word of God, I know it's tight, but it's still right. The Bible can't lie, because it is the unadulterated Word of God. My Bible also states that before His Word be made a lie, heaven and earth will pass away. Now as far as I know we're still standing here, so God's Word is still true. You feel me, Kiyah?"

I felt like I was in church. "Yes Leon, I guess you're right."

Leon wiped his head and got down on one knee. "I wasn't prepared to preach another sermon tonight, Sister Kiyah, but since I did and did it especially for you, would you do me the honor of being my wife?"

I couldn't say a word. I felt like this was all just a dream.

"Kiyah, if you become my wife, I promise I will fill your life with laughter and happiness. You will have all of your heart desires. How would you like spending your weekends in different cities, shopping and wearing the finest things that money can buy? Would you like that, Kiyah?"

He was amazing, he was fine, had money and intelligence. Why me? "Yes," was all I could say.

"Then say you will be my wife. I know that this is all happening so fast for you Kiyah, but being an anointed man of God, I move by the spirit. In the spirit realm there is no consciousness of time. Will you be my wife, Kiyah? Once we get back home we can do it legally, okay, sweetheart?"

He looked so cute and God knows I could get used to all this high living. "Yes, Leon, I will be your wife, but I'm still not giving you none," I said hugging him tight.

Exhausted, Leon said, "Whew, I thought I was preaching my trial sermon, in my conclusion, Sis Kiyah, you gotta give me some, because the Bible says that it is not God's will that man should be alone and the Bible also says that the bedroom is undefiled. Now give Daddy some."

Leon was all over me and once he started caressing my inner thighs and fondling my breast my body gave in to the temptation. We made love all night long or should I say all morning long. The sun was coming up by the time we finished. After prying my body from Leon's tight embrace, I was getting out the bed to take a shower. "Kiyah, where are you going?" Leon asked with his eyes half closed.

"I'm going to take a shower," I said holding the cover over me, while I was trying to find my pajamas on the floor.

"Why are you going to take a shower now? Come on baby, lay back down here with Daddy, I want to hold you."

Lord, have mercy, this man was so fine and he looked so good laying there with those sleepy eyes talking bout he wanted me to come back to Daddy.

"Leon, it's only going to take me five minutes to take a shower."

Leon looked so cute; trying to stay awake, he should have just closed his eyes and went to sleep. Some men just don't like to admit it, when a woman puts them out.

"Okay baby, I'll be waiting for you, hurry up," Leon said grabbing the remote control."

Once in the bathroom, I couldn't help but think about what had happened. Every time I thought about Leon looking into my eyes while he was making love to me, chills just went up and down my spine. Lord, I think I'm in love. I had never fallen for someone so quickly. He even told me he loved me a couple of times while we were making love. Ooh, the man made up for lost time. I checked my watch it was already after six in the morning. I hopped in the shower and let the water soothe me, and then I lathered up with my Love Spell shower gel, rinsed and jumped right out the shower. I knew Leon was waiting for me so I came out the bathroom with my towel wrapped around me. Once I got near the bed, just as I thought, I noticed that Leon was sound asleep. I slipped on a nightgown and climbed in bed with him. As I got in, he pulled me close to him, wrapped his arms around me and snuggled his face deep into my breast.

I woke up Saturday afternoon. I looked over and Leon was already gone. I sat up in bed and wiped my eyes. The door that connected our rooms was now shut, but it was open when we went to sleep that morning. I reached over, grabbed my cell and called Leon to see where he was. I got his voicemail on the first ring. At first I was annoyed, he could have left a note or something. But before I could get upset, Leon came walking through the door that lead to his room, fully dressed with a tray of food in his hand. "Good morning beautiful, is Daddy's baby hungry? Lord, knows you should be after last night," he said laughing while he lifted the silver lid up to display a plate of hot buttered pancakes, eggs and bacon. There was fresh fruit and orange juice and hot water for tea.

"Leon, I am starved, thank you. I did build up quite an appetite this morning," I said jokingly and reached forward to give him a kiss on the lips. Leon's phone started ringing and he spent the whole time I was eating my breakfast on the phone, one call after another. Once I finished eating, I left Leon in the room and went into the bathroom to take a shower. When I came out the shower I came into the room with my towel wrapped around me. Leon was still on the phone when I came out.

As I was in the closet trying to decide on what I was going to wear, I heard him tell the person he was talking to, "Listen, Bishop, I got some very important business I need to take care of right now so let me get back to you." He continued, "Alright, Bishop, anytime, God bless."

I decided to wear a Chinese style dress with the mules to match. I just felt like being comfortable, but at the same time still sharp. I liked the way this dress fit my shape. Still with the towel wrapped around me I reached into the drawer to get some underwear. "Kiyah, come here," he said.

"Okay, give me a minute, I want to put my clothes on," I answered.

Leon got up out the chair he was sitting in and walked over to me. "Kiyah, I've got workshops to do this afternoon. Why don't you give me a little inspiration," Leon said while he was unraveling my towel. "Kiyah, you are a beautiful woman," he said while looking at my naked body.

"Thank you, Leon. Why don't we wait until tonight?" Leon immediately started guiding me over to the bed.

"You have such big beautiful breasts and I'm a breast man. I can't help myself. I need you Kiyah, right now." Once he started using his tongue to caress my breasts, I could no longer resist. This was definitely my weakness. Once again it was on like popcorn. Leon was a good lover, but very demanding. Whew, within an hour I was completely worn out. This time it was Leon who was up and in the shower as soon as we were finished. I needed to take a nap. When Leon came out of the shower, he shocked me; he was just walking around naked as he was talking to me. He didn't think anything of it.

"Kiyah, I need to be at the Convention Center shortly, I will probably be gone all day. What do you want to do?"

Exhausted I told him, " I don't know, Leon, I'm not sure, I guess I would like to sight see. You know it would be nice to see something besides this bed in Dallas."

Leon laughed. He was walking around my room with his manhood swinging all around as he was gathering his things. "Okay, sweetheart, I will arrange that, one of my guys will give you a call around six, I guess you should be ready around then, is that okay?"

Wow, I like a man who takes charge like that.

"Yes baby, I will be ready at six and thank you honey, you are so good to me." Leon came over to the bed to give me a kiss. I knew that this wasn't just a kiss but also an exit.

"Okay, Kiyah, I've got to go, but keep the credit card I gave you yesterday, just in case you want to pick up some souvenirs or something for your kids while you're out. Our plane leaves at seven in the morning, so if you don't pick up something tonight, you probably won't get the opportunity to do so."

Leon walked off completely naked into his room, this time with the door open. Quickly I jumped up to take yet another shower, so that I could be comfortable taking my nap. After my shower, I was out like a light. I didn't bother getting my get out of jail free card, I didn't pass go, I went right to sleep.

I woke up when I heard the phone ring. It was Leon's phone ringing in the next room. I answered the phone, "Hello." Now, I know I'm saved and I know I shouldn't be answering his phone BUT I'm a black woman and I'm answering this darn phone to see just who's calling him.

"WHO IS THIS?" the voice on the other end of the phone said.

"This is his wife, WHO IS THIS?" I said to the woman who had not yet identified herself.

"Oh, I'm sorry, I didn't know you came with him," she said in a more polite tone.

"What do you mean, you didn't know I came with him, who is this?"

The person on the other end didn't say a word, I heard breathing then she hung up. I was really upset now. Leon was going to have to answer to this. I marched into my room, grabbed my cell phone and dialed his number. The phone rang four times before he answered. "Hello sweetheart, is something wrong?" he said in a very low tone almost like a whisper.

"Yes, there is, who did you give your hotel room number to?" I asked. "WHAT...what are you talking about? I'm five minutes away from teaching God's Word and you call me up with some foolishness." Leon was annoyed and he was now raising his voice. Well, I wasn't going to let him off that easy.

"Listen, Leon, a woman called your room and she had the nerve to say she didn't know I came with you, who is she?"

Leon was laughing now. "She didn't tell you her name?" he asked.

I really didn't think it was funny. "No," I said wondering why he went from being angry to being amused.

"Listen sweetheart, there has to be at least a few thousand women that heard me preach last night and I'm sure that one of those young ladies got their hopes up high. You know, I'm an alright looking dude and I'm anointed, some women get aroused by that. All Christians aren't saved, now if you're going to be with me, you are going to have to learn how to deal with these things." He continued, "I don't know who that was that called and I didn't give anyone my room number, I'm with you and, Kiyah, I Love You."

I was blushing all over myself by now and before I could stop myself. I said, "I love you too."

Leon sighed and said, "Okay, baby, it's after four, why don't you start getting ready, the guys will be picking you up soon and I'll try to get back early enough to take you to a late dinner, somewhere special."

Immediately I said, "Okay" and we hung up. I couldn't help thinking about the lady on the phone and the audacity she had to ask me who I was. Maybe what Leon said was true, anyhow I was the one with his Platinum Card. The rest of the evening went off without a hitch. The fellas picked me up at six just as Leon said and we went sight seeing. I picked up some souvenirs for the kids. We didn't get back to the hotel until ten-thirty. Paul informed me that Leon wouldn't be making it back in time to take me to dinner. He asked me if I would like to have dinner with him and the other guys, but I declined. Our flight was leaving early the next morning, so I wanted to get packed. I told Paul that I would order some room service. Which I did and while I was waiting for my food, I decided to call Queen Bee.

"Hey Queen, what's going on in Jersey?"

"Kiyah, why are you just calling me?"

"Girl, let me tell you, I've been shopping, and he gave me his credit cards and let me go on a shopping spree."

"I know you bought your sista something."

I bought her some shoes from Allure, one of her favorite designers, but I was going to surprise her when I get home. "Girl, I didn't have time for all of that, besides he sent his assistants with me. Anyway, I didn't tell you the mega news yet." Queen Bee was all in it now.

"What, tell me girl." "Queen, he is a pastor, a pastor girl, he has a church in Jersey and from what I hear, he can preach. That's what he's out here in Dallas doing. He was asked to speak for one of the biggest churches out here."

My sister was screaming in the background, Queen was telling my other sister Ever-Ready, what I was telling her. "What's his name again? I'm going to ask Trina about him, she knows all the ministers on the high circuit."

Yeah, I know she does, Trina was the assistant to Pastor Hall's wife, and he had a very large and thriving ministry in

Central Jersey. He was always having big-time ministers from across the United States at his church.

"Okay, ask Trina. His name is Leon Booker and let me know. I've got to go. We're leaving at seven in the morning. Have you heard from the kids?"

"Girl, your kids are in my den watching television, they didn't stay with their father two hours before they were calling me to come get them. Anyway, they're fine. Ever-Ready came over and baked some turkey wings soaked in Italian dressing and some macaroni and cheese. I made some turnip greens, white rice and corn-bread, so they ate that. These kids need to eat some fresh vegetables. I had to go down to Irvington Center and get them some clothes for church tomorrow, cause you didn't pack any church clothes."

My sister is just like our mom, as she was talking about cooking and going to get the kids some clothes, tears started welling up in my eyes. I missed my mom, but I was blessed to have a family that looked out for one another. My mom left a strong legacy in us. What Queen Bee did was something that Mommy would have done. When Mommy didn't like the way one of her grandkids were dressed or the way any of the kids looked, she would fuss a little, but she would immediately call her girls up and we would go shopping.

"Thanks Queen, I didn't send any church clothes with them because I knew they're father wasn't going to take them to church and Kyaisia has her house keys anyway. You could have taken them by the house to get their church clothes instead of going out to buy some."

Queen Bee sighed. I could tell she was exhausted from cooking. "Child please, I wasn't going through all of that. They needed some clothes anyway. I must have bought them at least ten outfits a piece. Kaseem wanted some type of Air Force sneakers. I told him he betta join the Air Force when he gets older." She laughed, and then said, "Girl, we had to go to three different stores before we found them. Everybody was sold out. I need some stock in those things."

I made a mental note to get Kaseem, for worrying Queen Bee about some sneakers. I had just bought him some sneakers two weeks ago.

"Queen, tell the kids I love them. I've got to go. I think I hear Leon coming down the hall," "Okay bye," I listened intensely for Leon to come into his room. But instead, I heard knocking at my door, after looking through the peephole, I realized it was the room service I ordered. Disappointedly I took my food and told the waiter to charge it to Leon's room.

After eating, I noticed it was well after midnight and Leon hadn't come back to his room yet. I was beginning to become annoyed. First, this unknown woman is calling his room, then, he's been gone all day and night without a trace. I decided to make the most of my last night in Dallas and get into the Jacuzzi. The whirlpool did the trick. My mind, body and soul were relaxed. After my bath, I packed to return home. As I was packing, I heard voices coming from next door. I moved closer to the door in order to hear, it was Leon's voice. He was having a conversation with someone. But I could not make out exactly what he was saying. It had something to do with money, I kept hearing him say that he would not be coming back because he wasn't done right. Out of pure frustration, I decided to get a glass, so that I could make out what was going on. Once I put the glass to the door, I locked it from my end, so that he couldn't open it on me without warning.

Now that I had the glass to the door I could hear complete sentences. Leon was upset and he was yelling, "I raised over forty thousand dollars cash tonight, never mind the checks, I know I did. Did you see how many people were in the $100 dollar line? It was at least three hundred people and way more than three hundred people in the $50 dollar line and he's going to tell me that my fifty percent (50%) cut is twelve thousand dollars. Church folk will rob you every time. How much was the speaker's offering James?" Leon said seemingly very agitated.

A male's voice said, "Pastor, it was four thousand seven hundred and twenty seven dollars and fifty-two cents cash, the checks total was three thousand four hundred and twenty five dollars, which we turned into Bishop to deposit into his account and forward you the funds once they clear." James continued, "Also, Pastor, it was three hundred and thirty seven people in the one hundred dollar line. Mark counted the fifty-dollar line and he reported five hundred and ninety two. That would amount to roughly sixty three thousand and three hundred dollars. There were at least fifteen thousand more people that gave unspecified amounts in the offering. So your estimated take, Pastor, should have been somewhere roughly at thirty five thousand or better without your speaker's offering."

I'm thinking wow, it's like that; that's a lot of money. Leon just went on ranting and raving about how he was cheated and how he wouldn't be coming back to Dallas to preach anymore. Once I heard him tell the guys that he was going to take it down and get packed for the trip back home, I decided to remove myself from the door, unlock it and pretend to be sleep. Somewhere while pretending to be sleep, I actually fell asleep. I had expected Leon to come in shortly after the guys had left, but when the alarm woke me up at five o'clock in the morning, I realized that Leon hadn't come to the room at all. I decided to go into his room to see if he was okay. To my surprise, not only was he not in his room, his bed hadn't been slept in all night as well. Maybe this money situation had bothered him more than I initially thought. On second thought, "WHERE IN THE HELL WAS HE?" He really better have a good explanation for not sleeping in his room last night. Just as I was about to check the closets for his luggage, my room phone rang. I rushed over to answer it. "Hello," I said hoping it was him.

"Kiyah, this is Leon, we're going to be leaving for the airport in thirty minutes, so get your things ready and the guys will be up to assist you. I will see you at the airport. My things are already down stairs." I guess he thought it was just that easy, oh but wasn't.

"Leon, where are you? Where have you been?" I said, worried.

"Listen, Kiyah, I don't like to be questioned. You're getting a little too comfortable with that, so let's get that under control now okay sweetheart, I'm where I'm at and I've been where I was okay."

Oh no, he didn't he got the wrong one this time. "Leon, who do you think you're talking to? First of all, if you don't feel as though I can question you after you were gone all night, then maybe we don't need to be together. Secondly, you can preach all this wife stuff to me one night and then the next night you're no where to be found. If you're going to preach something, baby doll, you better be prepared to live it. Lastly, I was worried because I hadn't heard from you, but now I'm mad because you've got the nerve to be sarcastic. Maybe you are up to no good. Maybe you were with the young lady that was calling your room. I don't know, but I tell you what, if you plan on continuing this relationship Mr. Booker YOU WILL show me a lot more respect. You don't just take it upon yourself to disappear without a trace and don't even bother sending me a message or leaving a note."

At that point I was really regretting everything that happened between us, but experiencing deep feelings for him all at the same time. Things moved really too fast between us. Leon's reply was not sarcastic this time at all and just like day and night he went from being sarcastic to sweet.

In a more subtle tone he said, "Everything is fine and it will be fine if you learn and understand that you don't need to question me. I love you, Kiyah, and I wouldn't do anything to hurt you. I had some things I needed to work out last night before we left for Jersey this morning. I'm on my way to the airport now, because I stayed at the Bishop's mansion last night and it is closer to the airport, okay," he said mildly.

Maybe he was straightening out his money situation. I thought I might have jumped the gun by getting upset and accusing him. "Okay, Leon, I didn't mean to accuse you of anything. I apologize and I will see you at the airport."

Once I hung up with Leon, I gathered all my things to prepare them for the bellhop. Within twenty minutes Paul was at my door to escort me downstairs to the car that was waiting. I didn't say much the whole ride to the airport, I was anxious to see Leon. Once we arrived at the airport, Paul checked my bags in, while the other guys and myself waited in front of the gate. "Are you okay, Sister Kiyah," Brother Tee said.

"I'm fine," I replied.

Tee continued, "I just wanted to make sure, cause you seem a little disturbed."

I said, "Oh, no I'm not disturbed, it's early and I'm anxious to get back home." But really I was disturbed, what have I done by sleeping with Leon, at the time it seemed like the right thing to do but now I didn't feel so good about it. Things really had moved too fast between us, and now I'm dealing with all of these crazy emotions.

Before you knew it, Leon had arrived and was acting as if nothing ever happened. He shook hands with the guys, then came over to me and gave me a quick hug and kiss on the cheek. I thought that was a little formal, but didn't think that it was cause for me to make a big deal out of it. After making small talk with the guys Leon called over to me,

"Kiyah, would you like anything from the concession stand, gum, candy or some reading material for the flight?"

I didn't want anything, I wanted him to come over and talk to me. I wanted to discuss what happened between us. There were some questions I needed to make sense of, for instance, this so-called marriage. "No, I don't need anything thank you," I said. He nodded to acknowledge that he heard me but just kept talking to the guys. Looking at my watch and noticing that we still had at least an hour before the flight left, I decided to pull out a book I had bought from a Christian bookstore in the mall. I found a seat close to the gate we were departing from and started to read. I must have been reading for at least thirty minutes, when I felt the presence of someone sitting right next to me, it was Leon.

"Kiyah, sweetheart, I know I haven't said much to you, since we've been in the airport this morning, but I need you to understand that a lot of people from the conference are traveling back to the respective states and towns they reside in. So, therefore I must be very careful with my conduct concerning you in public and especially here. I don't want anyone to get the wrong idea and start spreading rumors or anything. I have to protect what I have, Kiyah. I hope you understand that."

Why must he come over here and bother me with all of his lame excuses.

"Okay, Leon, you tell me what the wrong idea is? Explain that to me."

He seemed a little nervous and was looking all around and over his shoulder as if he was trying to hide from someone. "Kiyah, baby, could we discuss this later, okay I assure you that it will not always be like this, soon we will be able to tell everyone about our relationship, but not right now okay."

I didn't even respond, I didn't say one word.

So Leon continued, "Sweetheart, don't be upset okay. We will talk about this on the plane okay, Kiyah, please answer me."

I didn't say anything because I was too angry to answer. Leon kept trying to get through to me. "Kiyah, I promise I'm going to make this up to you, whatever you want okay, just tell me what you want and I will get it for you. I don't want to lose you, but I can't have you getting an attitude every time we are presented with a situation such as this, okay baby, don't do me like this."

What Leon failed to realize was, I didn't want anything materialistic. I had fallen for him in some sort of way. It was too soon to say whether or not it was love, but it was definitely something and all I needed from him was his heart. So just to get him away from me I decided to respond. "Look, Leon, I don't want anything from you. I just don't like this, why can't you have a friend or a girlfriend? Yes you may be a pastor, but you're single, so what's wrong with having a female companion?"

Leon continued to look around and back over his shoulder before answering me. "There's nothing wrong with it, Kiyah, but you have to understand that if we're traveling together for overnight stays people are going to assume that we are engaging in premarital sex and that will be unacceptable for a man in my position, now please try and understand that this is hard for me as well. People will not understand the commitment we made before God. Don't you think it's difficult for me to be looking and admiring you without being able to hold and caress you? You're a beautiful woman and what man wouldn't mind showing you off, but I have to think about my ministry and my church first, Kiyah, those people depend on me and I can't let them down. Try and understand."

Once again everything Leon was saying made sense to me. "Okay, Pastor, I understand, now you can go back over with the guys and I will see you on the plane."

Leon smiled and whispered, "Thanks, Kiyah, I love you." Not waiting for me to reply he got up and went over there where Paul and the rest of the guys were standing and continued to talk, every now and then people passing by would recognize him and stop to talk with him for a minute.

Finally, they announced the boarding of our flight. What a relief, I was more than ready to be heading home. When they called for the First Class section, I was the first one on. I must have been sitting there approximately ten minutes before Leon boarded the plane. He sat down next to me, grabbed my hand, and just held it, leaning back in his seat with his eyes closed. That's all he did for approximately an hour into the flight, I believe he had drifted off to sleep. He woke up when the flight attendant served our food. I did not care for any, but I took it any way and just let it sit there. "Kiyah, you're not going to eat anything sweety what's wrong?" Leon said while rubbing his hand on my leg.

"No, I'm not hungry. Leon, I really want to discuss this marriage or whatever we have," I said while purposely not looking at him. Leon seemed to be a little uncomfortable once I mentioned this topic, but I knew it was something we needed to discuss. I'm no fool, I know we're not truly married, but I was hoping he could really do or say something to convince me the way he did the other night. In my spirit, I was feeling so guilty and unsure of my salvation.

Leon grabbed my hand and squeezed it. "Listen sweetheart, I meant every word that I said to you the other night, I don't want you to think that I just did all of that just to get you in bed. I would never do that. I am an anointed man of God, I would never deceive you like that, Kiyah. Everything I said to you can be backed up by scripture."

Leon seemed to relax a little, but I could tell that he really didn't want to continue the conversation.

"Well, Leon I don't know. The Bible also says that we should live by the laws of the land. So we're supposed to get a license and do things in the proper way according to the governmental laws."

I could tell that this excited him. He sat up in his chair, leaned over closer to me, and said, "That's true, Kiyah, in those days before Christ that was true, but now we are no longer under the law. We are now under Grace. The Bible also declares that so as a man thinketh, so is he. Therefore, I think that I was spiritually married to you, although with my church and everything that surrounds my ministry, we have to take certain precautions and do things in a timely fashion, in our hearts, which are what God searches we are committed to one another. Is that alright Kiyah, because I can go on and on but I would rather not? I think that now is the appropriate time for us to discuss our living arrangements," Leon said shifting into a more comfortable position.

I thought that this would be a good time to interject. "Leon, I know that you feel very strongly about what you're saying, and I was going to try to think about our relationship in that manner, however, I would not feel comfortable having you stay or spend the night at my house with my children. They don't even know you."

Leon smiled very softly, while grabbing for my hand. "Alright, Kiyah, I can respect that and actually I was thinking the same thing. However I will assist you in anyway I can financially." He continued, "And you're absolutely right, we are not married, but God knows the desires of our hearts and he knows that I have very good intentions with you, Kiyah, and if things work out, I could definitely see marriage in our future."

He was on a roll now and for some reason I could not see marriage in my future. I had just gotten out of a bad marriage and was in no rush to get into another one. Still Leon continued, "Kiyah, keep this in mind, as my woman, I expect you to be available when I call, I understand that you have children, but always have a babysitter on standby so that when I need to be with you, I can."

What was he talking about? "What do you mean, Leon?" I said sounding confused.

Instantly he was very serious and replied, "When I am in the area ministering or nearby or I may be traveling outside of the state and I would like the pleasure of my woman's company afterwards, before or in between. I need to be sure that you can make yourself available. Can you handle that, Kiyah?"

Leon was very demanding and very up front. The problem was I didn't know if I could handle all of it. "I don't know, Leon, that's a lot of responsibility. I would not be able to guarantee you anything. I have children, they come first and babysitters cost money."

I must have told a joke and didn't know it because Leon was laughing out loud then he replied, "Please, Kiyah you're my woman. Money will no longer be a concern of yours. It's so cute, that you don't realize who I am and because of that it makes me want to give you more," he said looking deep into my eyes and then continued. "So don't even worry about the money, as a matter of fact have her to come and stay with you at your house around the clock and give her weekends off and I will pay her a weekly salary. Would two hundred dollars be enough?"

Boy, this was my kind of man. 'Lord *you've got to help me because I see myself being reeled right in.*' I answered, "Yes, but you don't have to do that, Leon. That's too much."

He stopped me before I could elaborate. He put his finger up to his lips as if to tell me to hush and said, "Listen, Kiyah, I make over five hundred and fifty thousand dollars a year on the road, I don't even need to take money from my own church if I didn't want to. In fact, my traveling ministry supports my church. I just remodeled my whole church and paid for it cash okay, sweetheart, so don't worry about money. Besides, her being there around the clock makes things more convenient for me. Therefore, when I call or come to pick you up it won't be too hard for you to leave. We can sneak away to the Airport Marriott or the Sheraton Tara on late nights and you can be back home in the morning before your kids awake."

It sounded good and those were very expensive hotels, but what I really wanted him to do was map out how he was going to get to know my children better. Anyway, he went on about how he was going to give me an allowance of one thousand dollars a month to help me out with my bills. Trust me this was more than what I expected. I was falling into something. I still couldn't call it love, but it was definitely something. The rest of the flight we were very affectionate towards one another. Kissing, hugging and snuggling. Leon kept telling me how much he loved me and I in return told him back. Even though I couldn't honestly say that I loved him yet in my heart; I knew that very soon I would.

Chapter Six

Back Home

Once we arrived in Newark the guys got my luggage while Leon and I stood and talked. We discussed getting together on Tuesday for dinner. I offered to accompany him to his church this morning because I was anxious to hear him speak, but he adamantly declined. He did not feel it was an appropriate time to introduce me to his congregation. After the guys retrieved my bags, we waited outside the baggage claim area for Miles.

"Kiyah, I will have Miles take you to your car and I will give you a call before I minister, so make sure that you have your phone on okay sweetheart, because I need to hear your voice for inspiration," Leon said, while scanning his phone for missed calls.

"Okay, I think that's Miles coming around the curve, so thanks for a wonderful trip, I really enjoyed myself and I will talk to you soon," I said and proceeded to walk outside. Leon followed.

He walked up close to me and whispered in my ear, "Why did you walk away from me like that Kiyah. No hug? You can hug me in public okay?" At the same time, he was gesturing to Miles to get my things and put them in the trunk.

"Okay, Leon, I just thought that you would prefer not to do those types of things in public," I replied while giving him a warm and gentle hug. He had the widest smile on his face now, and immediately I proceeded to get in the truck. Miles had opened the door for me and Leon helped me in.

Before I could close the door he reached in and said, "You know, Kiyah, I am fascinated by you and I know that you are the one. The mere fact that you are considerate of my position and careful enough not to hug me in public shows me that you have an exceptional amount of potential. This excites me, Kiyah, and we can definitely go places. But just for future reference sweetheart, airports are okay for hugs but church functions are not. Now don't alarm yourself, we will definitely discuss the dos and don'ts at a later time. And don't worry, you will get the hang of it." Leon leaned in closer, gave me a kiss on my lips, and winked. "I will talk to you soon, Kiyah, I love you," he whispered while closing the door.

As Miles was pulling off I saw Leon walk back over to where Paul and the other guys were and he was slapping five and laughing. I wondered what that was all about?

Miles didn't say anything for the short drive to my car, but once we arrived, he turned to me and said, "How was your trip?" He shocked me.

"It was fine, Miles. I thought the cat had your tongue."

He laughed. "Naw, it's nothing like that. I know if Leon saw us talking he would give both you and I the third degree later. I just wanted to make sure everything went okay on the trip for you, Kiyah. I like your style and you seem like a very nice young lady and I don't want to see you hurt."

To see me hurt? Now why was he going there? I was curious now. "What makes you think I might get hurt, Miles?" I asked. Before answering my question, Miles hopped out the jeep and started getting my bags out. I got out of the jeep on my own and opened the trunk of my car so that he could place my bags inside.

"Miles, why won't you answer me?"

He stopped what he was doing, put my suitcase on the ground, looked up at me and said, "You know out of all of the woman I've seen come and go, you're different. There is something special about you. I always mind my business. That's what I get paid for. I get paid to drive and mind my business. I will be honest with you, Kiyah; I have a criminal past and I can't afford to lose this job. It will be very difficult for me to come across another one. But I'm going to go out on a limb here and say this, *everything is not always what it seems, so be careful.*" Miles was talking in riddles again and I didn't know what to think. Maybe Miles was attracted to me or something, but it was getting late and I wanted to drop my luggage off at home before going to church. So I gave Miles a hug and thanked him for helping me with my things and I reassured him that I would take everything he said into consideration.

I went home, dropped my luggage off, and headed down to the church. Sunday school would just be letting out. Before I made my way into the church, I decided to go to Dunkin Donuts to get a coffee and wheat donut. As I was getting back into the car, my cell phone started ringing. It was Leon. "Hey beautiful, what's going on," he enthusiastically said.

"Nuthin, I'm just leaving Dunkin Donuts and on my way to church," I said.

Leon then said, "I miss you already and I can't wait until Tuesday to see you so I was thinking, I have to speak at Bishop Johnson's church located in Newark this evening. Why don't you come down to hear me and we can get together afterwards, okay?"

I was thinking, *why not*? I really wanted to see him and I was anxious to hear him speak. "Sure, that sounds great. What time are you scheduled to be there?" I asked.

He quickly said, "Six o'clock. So I'll see you then." Leon hung up.

I headed back to the church and once I got there I located my children, who were in the kitchen eating. They always served breakfast for the Sunday school students.

"Hey Kyasia! Hey Kaseem!" I said with my arms stretched wide open awaiting their embrace. I thought Kaseem was going to knock me clear off my feet; he was so excited to see me. Kyasia was too; although she was more concerned with the souvenirs I had bought her. "Thanks for the gifts, Mom, but who did you go away with?" Kyasia asked.

I needed to get out of this line of questioning quick, fast, and in a hurry. "A friend, sweety, just a friend, I don't think you know them," I said and then started talking to some of the kitchen crew. Kyasia and Kaseem quickly finished their breakfast and went running about showing their things off to their friends. This was a relief, 'cause I didn't want little *Ms. Mini Me* (Kyasia) to give me the third degree. I ain't mad at her though, how could I be, she's just like me.

We were upstairs and in church before you knew it. Service was good but for some reason I couldn't get into it. I had a heavy feeling of anxiety on me. I guess I was anxious to hear Leon preach tonight.

After morning service, I gave my sisters their gifts and they both loved them. I told Benita about Leon being a minister and that I was going down to Bishop Johnson's church to hear him speak.

Benita quickly declared, "I'm going with you." Benita is something else, she never misses a beat.

"All right Benita, that's fine, but I'm leaving here at five thirty," I stated laying down the law. I wanted to get there early enough to find a parking space and a good seat. Of course, I went home to freshen up and change my clothes. I had to be sharp!

Once I returned to the church where some of the members were downstairs in the dining hall eating awaiting night service, I went straight over to Benita's table.

"Come on, Benita, let's go. It's five thirty and I don't want to be late," I said impatiently.

"Okay, okay, I'm ready. Just let me finish the last of my food," Benita said while stuffing some cornbread into her mouth.

"You don't need all of that fattening food anyway, wrap it up and save it for later. I've got to go," I demanded.

"Boy, you sure are pushy, Kiyah. You won't even give me a chance to finish eating."

"Benita, I'm sorry, but I've got to go. It's suppose to be crowded down there and I want to find a parking space and get a good seat. So please work with me or else you can just stay here," I replied knowing that the thought of her staying and missing out on experiencing some good gossip first hand would motivate her to stop feeding her face and prepare to leave.

"Okay, okay, I'm coming" Benita whined, while wrapping up her food.

We made it down to Bishop Johnson's church in ten minutes flat. I found a parking spot right in front of the church. It seemed as though the crowd hadn't arrived yet. After entering the sanctuary, I noticed that I had my choice of seats. However, I opted to sit closer to the middle of the sanctuary, at the end of the pew closest to the isle.

In no less than twenty minutes the sanctuary was packed. As I looked around, I suddenly noticed that Sandy was sitting in the rear of the church. When she spotted me she gestured towards me with a smirk on her face.

"Benita, not now, but in a minute, turn around and look toward the door, but look to the left. Sandy's sitting back there." Of course

154

Benita couldn't wait. Immediately she turned around and waved at Sandy.

"Benita, WHAT IS YOUR PROBLEM? I asked you to wait," I said very annoyed with her.

"Kiyah, stop being so paranoid. There's nothing wrong with me speaking to Sandy, but why does she have that look on her face," Benita said.

"You saw it too? I wonder what her problem is." I asked.

"I don't know, but she did mention one or two times that she knows your friend Leon and she would immediately start laughing," Benita informed me.

"I'm not thinking about Sandy. Let her tell it, she knows everybody. Do I look okay?" I asked.

"You look fine," Benita said.

Looking around I noticed that the praise leaders were taking their place in the front of the sanctuary indicating that service was about to begin. I didn't see Leon or any of his boys anywhere in sight.

One of the praise team leaders asked everyone to be seated and settle downy because service was about to begin. They opened up with *Lord I Want to Be a Sanctuary*. There was a sweet spirit in the place. You could feel the presence of the Lord. At least at first I did, but I couldn't keep Sandy and that sinful smirk on her face out of my mind the implications of her stating that she knew Leon only added to my guilt. It seemed as though everyone in the building was in a high praise except for me, including Sandy.

The praise team finished up and proceeded to take their seats while they continued worshipping and praising God for His presence. Two of the members of the praise team broke out in a shout and that started a snowball effect all over the building. People everywhere took to the isles to cut a step. Even Sandy got her praise on. I felt too convicted to give my God the type of praise He deserved. I was too concerned that Leon was somewhere watching and might see me; or that Sandy and her crew were waiting for me to do something for them to talk about. However, the main reason was my guilt. I waved my hand and stomped my feet, but I definitely realized that I had lost my dance.

Once the praise diminished, the few people still in the midst of their praise were seated by the ushers. The others were being ushered out.

Bishop Johnson got up from his chair and approached the podium. At the microphone he said, "Would everyone please stand as we receive the Man of God for this evening as he enters the sanctuary."

Everyone stood and turned towards the aisle and Leon accompanied by six gentlemen, (*the same guys that went to Dallas with us*) came strutting down the center aisle. Leon had on a dark gray pinstriped tailored-made suit. The other five guys wore solid colored suits.

Leon and Paul went straight to the pulpit; the other five gentlemen sat on the front row. Once Leon was seated, Bishop Johnson, in a loud voice said, "Praise the Lord, saints of God we are in for a treat tonight. I thank God for Pastor Leon Booker. This young man can deliver a powerful Word. But before he comes before you, the choir will render us a selection and since he is on a heavy schedule, he asked that I refrain from a formal introduction and just let him come forth after the choir and give us what thus saith the Lord. Is that all right?"

Everyone replied with a resounding, "AMEN!" Bishop Johnson continued, "Praise the Lord. We will now hear from the choir and immediately after the choir the next voice you will hear will be that of PASTOR LEON BOOKER, let's receive them both with a hearty amen."

Everyone in the building again shouted, "AMEN!"

The choir sang to the glory of God and immediately following, Leon got up and greeted everyone very eloquently. He spotted me in the crowd and winked at me. I thought that this was very risky on his part; however, no one else seemed to notice. Leon's spoke on relationships. How ironic?

The congregation was so uplifted and taken by the words that were coming out of his mouth. He was without a doubt anointed. People were shouting and praising God all over the sanctuary fifteen minutes into his sermon. I however felt as if he was speaking directly to me. Once or twice in his sermon, he even said my name. For instance he would say, "You understand what I'm saying Sista Kiyah, I know you're with me." I was so surprised that he would take a chance at doing this in front of all of these people.

Anyway, the man preached the house down. I was totally amazed and it strengthened my attraction towards him. Benita was crying and praising God. I don't even think she noticed that Leon had said my name several times during his sermon. You know the Holy Spirit had to have hold of her for her not to have had her antennas up, nosey as she is. Once Benita had calmed down and got her self together, I informed her that I wanted to leave. Leon was winding up his message and had started encouraging the people to sow a seed offering.

I really needed to get the kids home and to bed.

"Benita are you ready?" I asked.

"Hallelujah, thank You Jesus," was all Benita could say. I stood up and got ready to leave, knowing that once Benita came out the Spirit, she would immediately come outside when she noticed that I was gone.

As I stood up and put my pocketbook on my shoulder, Leon stopped right in the middle of his call for a seed offering and said into the microphone, "Kiyah don't leave yet, sit down."

Shocked, I turned around to see if anybody noticed before I sat down and of course, Sandy was looking dead in my face with that devilish grin on her face. Everyone else was still slayed in the Spirit. Some people were crying while rocking themselves back and forth. Others were laid out on the floor covered with white sheets.

Suddenly Leon instructed, "Ushers, please help my brothers and sisters up off the floor and into their seats. I don't want them to be excluded from this blessing." The ushers did as he had requested and within minutes he continued, "Brother, come here." Leon pointed to a surprised young man sitting in the third row on the right hand side of the sanctuary. Once the young man came up to Leon, he reached into his pocket, took out a knot of money, plucked off a crisp one hundred dollar bill, and placed it into the young man's hand.

Then he began to explain, "I seeded one hundred dollars into this man's life and I don't want anything from him. See, I expect something back from God. Lord if you keep me in good health, Lord if you protect my children, that's all I want You to bless me with. See, some folks want to receive financially, but I want God to bless my home and bless my children. Now, everyone in the house that is able, I want you to sow a hundred dollar seed into this ministry, not for me, but for Bishop Johnson's ministry. See I have to do what the Spirit is sanctioning me to do. I'm sorry if I'm offending anyone, but I MUST DO THIS! I'M SANCTIONED to do what the Spirit moves me to do. Now I don't want any one to miss out on their blessing. The Bible declares that it is more blessed to give than to receive. The spirit is saying that there is a need in this house and God wants to bless you if you have faith that he will return it to you a hundred folds. I'm not going to beg you to be blessed. Everyone that can sow a hundred dollar seed offering into this ministry, not for me, but for this ministry, bring it now," Leon exclaimed.

To my surprise, at least twenty or more people were walking up to the front of the church with a hundred dollars in their hands and dropping it at the altar.

Once they brought the money up, Leon instructed them to form a line down the center of the aisle. Then Leon continued, "Thank you, may God bless you. I know that there are some people here, who don't have a hundred dollars to give, but the Lord still wants to bless you, so if you have fifty dollars and that's all you can afford to give, you can come now. God has no respect of persons; he will honor your fifty dollars as a hundred if that's all you have to give."

Immediately even more people, at least seventy-five, walked up to the altar and dropped their fifty dollars on it. Then he had them all to line up as well so that he could pray for them. They were falling out like dominos as he laid hands on them. It was getting late now and I really needed to go.

So as Leon was calling for everyone with twenty dollars, I decided to ease out. Benita pulled me back.

"Kiyah why are you rushing, I've got twenty dollars and I want to get prayed for," Benita said. She was really taken by his preaching. I had to admit that he was one of the best that I had ever heard. Yet it seemed so strange for me to hear him and feel anything knowing him the way that I did.

"Okay Benita, but you betta be the first one up there in line, because I really do have to go. I've got to get the kids. It's getting late and I'm starting to come down with something. I think I'm catching a cold or something," I said while sitting back down.

Benita bounced on out the row and down the aisle with her twenty dollars in hand and there must have been at least a hundred or more people in tow. Benita was the third person in line, and once Leon began to lay hands on the people ahead of her, she was already taken over by the Holy Spirit and into a high praise. So when he finally got to Benita, the minute he laid hands on her, she started shaking like she was having convulsions and fell out on the floor. It made me cry, just to think that finally the Holy Ghost had gotten a hold of her. Maybe she could finally be delivered from her nosiness.

Seriously, I was crying because the Lord was surely in this place and He came to heal, deliver and set free. You could see that He was doing just that all over the building. *'Lord I want and I need a blessing from you right now. I need to be healed. I know that this man is definitely used by you and I want to make sure that it's right and I need you to open up my mind to receive Your word and apply it to my life, as you see fit God. There's something in my spirit that makes me question my decisions lately. Lord, I need to know if that's you. Show me Lord, guide me and lead me in the direction You want me to go. Lord I want to do what's honorable and acceptable in Thy sight. Lord I know that You inhabit the praises of your people and Lord I need you to inhabit me. Lord God, give me my praise back.'*

As I finished, I noticed that Benita was up from off the floor and heading back to her seat. Once she reached our row, she asked me to pass her Bible and bag to her so we could leave. *'Thank you Jesus, that's one prayer answered,'* I thought.

Finally, we had made it to the car, and once inside, Benita could not stop talking about what had just taken place. "Child that man sure can preach. You've got to get him to come and preach at our church," she said excitedly. I didn't say a word. But I caught myself blushing every time she mentioned how talented Leon was.

Ten minutes later I dropped Benita off at our church to get her car. I then proceeded to get the kids from Queen Bee's and head home.

It took me only ten minutes to get from Queen Bee's house to my home. I instantly instructed the kids to take their baths and go ahead to bed.

Once the kids were asleep, I called Queen Bee and told her all about the night. She was so excited.

"Okay Kiyah, why don't you get him to speak for Men's Day next month at our church? Talk to him about it and let me know. But do it soon, so that we can get the flyers out in time," Queen said, sounding more and more excited. "Kiyah we could also have Sue-Sue to sing right before he comes up," Queen continued. As she was talking, my cell phone (the one Leon gave me) started to ring.

"Queen, I've got to go. That's him calling me. He must have gotten out of service. I'll call you back," I said rushing her off the phone.

"Okay, don't forget to ask him about Men's Day," Queen said before I hung up.

"Okay," I said while hanging up the phone.

I reached into my pocketbook and grabbed the cell phone that Leon had bought for me. "Hello," I said trying not to sound so anxious.

"Hello, sweetheart, why did you leave so soon?" Leon said with that oh, so sexy voice of his.

"I needed to get the kids to bed and besides I think I coming down with the flu or something," I said apologetically.

"Oh, baby I'm really sorry to hear that, How did you enjoy my sermon?"

162

"The Lord really used you in a mighty way and the people were immensely blessed," I said proudly.

"Yeah, I'm glad you enjoyed it. Did you catch it when I called your name while I was preaching," Leon said while laughing.

"Yes, I did. Why would you do something like that? I thought you didn't want to expose our relationship just yet."

"Kiyah, it's dangerous for people to give a man a microphone that knows what to do with it."

"What do you mean Leon? I don't understand," I said confused.

"Don't worry about that sweetheart, look I have to drop a few people off first, but then I would like to bring you some soup or tea to help you feel better," Leon said sounding concerned.

"Oh, no Leon you don't have to do that. I will be fine," I shot back.

"Kiyah, you looked incredible tonight and I really want to be with you, so can I come over to your house?" he asked.

"I don't think so Leon. My kids are here and I'm not sure that would be a good idea," I said reluctantly.

"Come on, Kiyah, what's the harm in sitting on the couch watching television. I just want to be with you. I miss you. What's the problem? By the time I get back in your area your kids should be sleep and I'll leave before they even know I was there," Leon said convincingly.

I finally gave in and gave him the directions to my house and then I immediately proceeded to make sure the house was tidy and neat. Thank God, the kids were already asleep. I freshened up and put on some jean Capri's and a tank top so that I could feel more comfortable.

Within an hour, Leon was calling me from outside my house and I opened the door for him. He had changed into a black velour sweat suit and black sneakers and was sporting a baseball cap to match. As he entered my house, he handed me a bag that contained some soup and crackers. "Thank you," I said as he handed me the bag. "You can have a seat in the living room. Would you like to watch some TV?"

Leon looked at me as I walked past him and over to the television. "No I don't want to watch television; do you have those cable channels that just play music on them," he said. He seemed tired.

"Yes I do. What do you want to hear, gospel?"

"No, as a matter of fact put it on jazz, thanks," Leon replied, while sitting down.

Then he turned to me and said, "You have a nice place here Kiyah. I'm impressed. Why don't you go eat your soup and then come back in here and sit with me?"

"Why do I have to go eat my soup? I could just eat it here with you, is that okay?" I said, raising my eyebrow.

"Of course sweetheart, I just thought with the white carpet and all that you did not eat in this room," he said, throwing his hands up in a defense mode. He was absolutely right. I did not allow anyone to eat in my living room because I had white carpet and white over-sized furniture.

"I'm not a kid and I trust myself not to spill it," I said laughing as I sat down next to him and started to sip some of the soup. He had gotten me tomato soup, which I really didn't like, but I didn't want to be rude. So I sipped a couple of teaspoons and then discarded it in the kitchen sink and threw the container in the wastebasket. After throwing away the soup, I hollered into the living room and asked Leon if he wanted something to drink. He declined. I went into the bathroom next to the kitchen and brushed my teeth before going back into the living room.

When I finally got back into the living room, Leon was stretched out on the couch with his eyes closed and his feet planted on the floor. He was tired, but once he felt my presence he opened up his arms and extended an invitation for me to sit down next to him. As I did he immediately snuggled me into his arms and we fell asleep.

I woke up around five in the morning and I checked on the kids; they were still sound asleep. Leon was knocked out - he looked so sweet. This was refreshing, him just wanting to come over and be with me (no sex involved). Maybe he was sincere; after all, he would have to be the way that God used him. Finally, after sitting there thinking, it was now about five thirty and I decided to wake Leon up so that he could go home before the kids got up.

Before leaving, Leon gave me five hundred dollars. He said that he had raised approximately six thousand dollars at Bishop Johnson's church last night and half of that was his take plus his Speakers Offering. Hmm, if I heard him correctly, he had said that he was raising the offering for the ministry at that church. Oh well, I ain't gonna complain, not while it's benefiting me.

Then he asked me for a toothbrush and a washcloth. I always keep extra toothbrushes in the house. It took him all of fifteen minutes to get himself together before leaving. As I was walking him to the door, he pushed my body up against the wall, kissed me very intensely, and then said, "Kiyah this is the beginning of something wonderful. I love you and I'll call you later." He then headed to his car, got in, and drove off.

Later that day while I was at work, Leon called and I asked him about speaking for our Men's Day Program. He instantly replied, "I believe I have something scheduled on that day, but I will make some arrangements. You know I will do anything for you."

"Thank you, Leon. I'm going to need a picture and your bio for the programs and flyers okay."

"Sure, no problem sweetheart, give me your church address and I will have my secretary to send it out ASAP."

I gave him the information and told him that I had some work that I needed to do so I would give him a call later. Really, I wanted to call Queen and let her know that he had agreed to speak for our Men's Day. No sooner than I hung up with Leon, that's exactly what I did.

Queen was very pleased. She said that she had spoken to the president of our Men's Auxiliary. He knew of Leon and was overwhelmed that we were able to get him for that date. He said that he wouldn't have ever dreamed that we would be able to get him and asked her how in the world she got him to speak for us. Queen told him that we had an inside connection. We both laughed at that.

Two days later Leon's picture came to the church in the mail, but no bio. I made a mental note to question him about that when I spoke to him later. Everything was going fine in the office; even Sandy was being nice to me. Before you knew it, the day had whisked by. It was already lunchtime. I went out for lunch and called Leon. I asked him about the bio and, he stated that he would bring it to me when we got together on Friday. Leon had planned a romantic weekend for us. I was excited. Anyway, we didn't need the bio right away; we wouldn't need it until we were ready to make the programs for the service.

I went back to work after talking to Leon in my car for the entire lunch period. After work, I went home, fed the kids and took a nice hot bubble bath and went to bed early. Around 9:30p.m. my house phone began ringing in my ear. I know it wasn't Leon; he wouldn't call me on my house phone. As I checked the caller ID, I noticed it was Queen, so I decided to answer. "Hello," I said with a sleepy voice.

"Kiyah, WAKE UP!" Queen screamed into the phone.

"I'm awake. What's wrong?" I said sitting up in bed.

"Kiyah, I just got off the phone with Trina, from Bishop Hall's church and I was telling her about Leon coming to our church to speak for Men's Day. She told me that she knows him very well, that her pastor and Leon are good friends," she said giving me the whole run down.

"Okay, *and*," I said admonishing her to get to the point.

"AND she went on to say that when he comes to her church the women go crazy. I told her that he was liking you, and then she said that she thought he was still married."

I was numb. Did I hear her say STILL MARRIED? I couldn't say anything. Queen said, "Kiyah, don't get upset. Trina is going to find out and if he is, you know you're going to have to end it immediately. Do you hear me Kiyah?" Queen demanded.

"Yes I hear you. Queen, I don't think he's still married, he told me he was married but was divorced for quite some time now," I replied defensively.

Queen made one final statement before hanging up. "Well I'm going to get to the bottom of it, that's for sure. You go ahead back to sleep and I'm going to call Trina back and see what she's found out."

Before she could hang up I yelled, "Call me back." After Queen hung up I tried reaching Leon, but his voice mail kept picking up on the first ring. I couldn't sleep. I stayed up all night thinking. Maybe everything was just a misunderstanding. Besides, Queen never called me back. If she had found out anything else, she would have called me back. Oooh! I couldn't wait to speak to him.

Chapter Seven

Exposed

On my way to work, I dialed his number non-stop. Every single time without fail it immediately went to the voicemail. I decided to leave him a message. "Hi baby, this is Kiyah. I need to have a meeting with you up close and personal. Call me back," I said in a very sexy voice and then I left my number. I wanted to sound very sexy, first, to ensure that he would call me back right away, and secondly, to keep him from knowing that anything was wrong.

Once I reached work, I tried to keep myself busy and forget about what Queen had told me the night before, but I couldn't. Every minute I was checking the phone that Leon bought me to see if it was still on, trying to make sure that he could reach me. I was a nervous wreck and tense. To make matters worse, Sandy chose today of all days to tell me how she knows Leon. She said that his father could preach and both his brother and sister as well. She didn't say anything offensive so I couldn't be mad at her. I didn't want to ask her if she knew of him being married, so I just acted nonchalantly and proceeded to walk into my office and do some paperwork.

Towards the middle of the day, Queen called. "Kiyah, Trina called me back a few minutes ago, she said that he was married, but she doesn't think that him and his wife are still together."

"I didn't think he could still be married, not with all the time we spend together," I said relieved.

Queen hung up soon after that and I had calmed down a whole lot. It must have been after 4:00p.m. when my private cell phone rang; it was Leon. "Hey sweetheart, I know you were trying to get me, but I was preaching at a revival last night and I didn't turn my phone on until just now. I needed some rest," he said, so innocently.

"Oh, okay I was just worried that's all, I'm looking forward to seeing you tomorrow," I said quietly.

"Me too, Kiyah. I miss you," Leon replied in a very soft tone.

"Okay Leon, I've got to go. I will see you tomorrow," I said ready to hang up.

"Whoa, Kiyah, we haven't talked all day. What's wrong? This is not like you sweetheart. Is there something wrong? Talk to me."

I didn't want to mention anything about what Trina had said until tomorrow, but since he created the opportunity, I spoke up. "Yes, Leon as a matter of fact there is something wrong. A friend of mine that goes to Bishop Hall's church and has heard you speak there seemed to think that you were still married. Now I asked you in the beginning of our relationship if you were married," I said in a serious tone.

"Come on, Kiyah, I have two children and was married for quite a few years of course some people are going to think I am still married. I didn't advertise my divorce. A man in my position shouldn't. But I assure you sweetheart, I am not married to anyone but you," Leon said with conviction.

"Leon, we are not married, so stop that. I'm not comfortable with us sleeping together in the sight of God without that type of commitment," I said lowering my voice.

Leon was chuckling now. "Kiyah, you're a good girl and I admire that, but there is nothing wrong with what we're doing, I assure you. I'm a man of God, I wouldn't tell you anything wrong. See, what people fail to realize is that I am a preacher yes, but I'm also a man. I have needs like any other man. I fall short and God's grace is still sufficient. Everything is going to be fine sweetheart; you're just a little upset because of what you heard."

Maybe Leon was right. I might be a little upset but after talking with him, I felt better. In fact, I picked the kids up, went home, cooked a nice dinner, cleaned up, and later fell into a peaceful sleep.

Friday went by so quickly and that wasn't soon enough for me. I couldn't wait for the end of the day so that I could run home and get prepared to meet Leon. The kids' father picked them up from school and they were spending the weekend with him. I had the house all to myself. I blasted my Yolanda Adams CD while I was soaking in the tub. I kept my cell phone in the bathroom just in case Leon called. He didn't call while I was in the tub. As soon as I got out and as I was walking into my room to get dressed he called.

"Kiyah are you ready? I'm outside."

What does he mean he's outside? It was just a little after six and he wasn't supposed to be at my place until seven o'clock. "Leon, I thought you said you would be here by seven when we spoke yesterday," I said confused.

"I know, but I was already in the area, so I decided to come a little earlier. Just open the door for me. I'll watch a little bit of the news. I don't mind waiting until you're ready."

"Okay, I don't have any clothes on. Give me a minute, I'll be right down," I answered.

"Take your time," Leon shot right back.

So I slipped on my robe and ran downstairs to open the door for him and once he was inside, I gave him the remote control and ran upstairs to get dressed. I decided to put on some pale green pants with a short sleeve summer sweater to match. I pulled out some wedge-heeled sandals that matched and put them on. I fixed my hair, made up my face and then sprinkled on some of my Escada Sentiment perfume. Once I checked everything in the mirror and deemed it to be okay, I proceeded downstairs.

"Leon, I'm ready," I yelled halfway down the stairs.

"All right," he answered while meeting me at the bottom of the stairs. "Kiyah you look beautiful as always," he said admiring me.

"Thank you, Leon. I'm ready when you are," I said walking towards the door.

We left the house and I didn't have any idea where we were going. Leon loved to surprise me. This turned out to be a simple evening, however. First, we went to see a movie and then out to dinner at a Japanese steak house. Afterwards, we got a room at the Tara Sheraton in Parsippany and spent the night.

Saturday morning after breakfast, we walked around the grounds of the hotel then we sat downstairs in the lobby and talked. Later, Leon took me to Rockaway Mall to buy me some things to change into. We left the Mall and went back to our room at the Tara Hotel and frolicked around in the room for the rest of the evening. By midnight, Leon was dropping me off at home so that he could go and prepare himself to preach on Sunday morning.

For the next three weeks, the same scenario occurred every weekend; either a movie or Broadway play, dinner, and a room at one of the finest hotels in the area. Every weekend Leon would hand me no less than five hundred dollars and take me shopping. Everything was going great between us. We would talk several times a day. At least two nights out of the week Leon would come over to my house after the kids were sound asleep, and we would snuggle and watch television until the wee hours of the morning. I had totally gained confidence in him and really started gearing my mind towards a life with him. I was in love.

It was a Tuesday morning, the week before our Annual Men's Day. I woke up feeling great and Leon had just left at about five thirty in the morning. I would always set the alarm on my cell phone to wake us at 5:30a.m. in order to make sure he was good and gone before the kids woke up. Besides, it was very uncomfortable sleeping on the couch in a sitting position. I needed at least a good hour to an hour and a half of real sleep in my own bed.

It was now 7:00a.m. and I was preparing myself to leave and get the kids to school. I was really feeling comfortable with our relationship and happy. Lord, it was great being with a saved man of God. I couldn't help thinking about how reluctant I was in the past to get involved with a saved, Holy Ghost filled man. I thought that they were too stuffy, self-righteous and old fashioned. Boy was I wrong; Leon was wonderful, honest, and sweet and we really had a great time hanging out together.

My thoughts were interrupted when the kids came running downstairs yelling that it was time to go. After dropping the kids off at school as I normally did, I headed down to the job. I parked in my usual parking space and went straight to my office. I was early; almost 8:20a.m. and I wasn't due in until 9:00a.m. I was feeling so good that day, that nothing, not even Sandy, was going to get to me today. I even spoke to her and meant it.

"Hi, Sandy how are you today?" I said almost singing it.

"Fine, Kiyah, how are you?" Sandy said with a look of shock on her face.

"I'm doing great. Is Benita in yet?"

"No, she's not but she should be here any minute now," Sandy said pleasantly.

"Thanks," I said as I proceeded to walk past her to my desk and have a seat. I was busy with my paperwork, when Benita finally rolled her way into the office.

"KIYAH, WHAT ARE YOU DOING HERE? IT'S NOT EVEN NINE O'CLOCK YET!" Benita yelled over at me.

"I decided to get an early start at my paperwork today." I said singing again.

"Oh, that's good Kiyah. Did you finish the programs for the Men's Day next week yet? Cause Queen Bee wanted me to start making the copies," she said walking over towards my desk.

"No, I'm waiting on Leon's bio. I will call him in a little while and see if I can get it faxed over to us from his office."

"Just let me know. I don't want to wait too long. I get tired of always doing everything at the last minute," Benita said pushing the issue.

"All right, Benita, I will give him a call now," I said with a sigh.

At first, I felt a little uncomfortable calling Leon at this time in the morning. I knew that he had just left my house and was probably exhausted. But I knew that Benita was going to worry me too death until I got the programs finished. So I dialed his number from one of the lines on the church phone; it rang several times before his voice mail picked up. I left a message.

"Leon, this is Kiyah and I was wondering if you could possibly bring your bio past the house tonight or either have someone at your office to fax one to my office; the number is 555-0971. We really need it right away. The event is next week. I guess in all the time we've been spending together in the last three weeks, I should've mentioned it before now. But I guess I was preoccupied (I laughed). Nevertheless, I really enjoyed your company last night; we always have a good time when we're together. I just want you to know that I appreciate you and I miss you already. Give me a call back at my office in regards to your bio. The number is 555-0977. Love you, Bye," I said almost prying myself deep into my cubicle so that no one else in the office could hear my conversation.

I hung up and pushed my chair all the way out into the aisle so that Benita's desk was within my view. "Benita, I called him and hopefully if I receive the information I need, the programs will be finished by the end of the day," I yelled across the room.

"Okay, Kiyah. Thanks. I'll be over there in a minute," Benita yelled back.

I was busy at work when Benita walked over to my desk at least twenty to twenty-five minutes later. "What's up, Kiyah, Giiiirrrrllll did you know that everyone around here is bussing over the Men's Day next week. Everyone is anxious to hear Pastor Leon Booker speak," Benita said sounding so excited.

"Yes, Benita, I know all of the members of the church are talking about it. I know that they are going to have a good time in the Lord next Sunday, because the Lord surely uses him in a mighty way," I said proudly.

"You got that right! I felt the Holy Ghost all over that place last month down at Bishop Johnson's church," Benita said while trying to cut a little step in front of my desk. As Benita was running her mouth about the service we attended at Bishop Johnson's church approximately three weeks ago, Sandy interrupted her. "Kiyah you have a call from Pastor Booker's office on line three," Sandy said, her eyebrows raised.

"Okay Sandy, put them on hold and I'll pick it up in a second," I said and then turned to Benita. "This is probably his secretary, prayerfully she will be sending the bio momentarily." I said while picking up line three. "Hello, Kiyah speaking," I said in my most professional tone.

"Kiyah, I'm calling from Pastor Leon Booker's office did you just leave a message on his service?" the woman's voice on the other line asked.

"Yes I did," I said in a confused tone.

"Well, this is his WIFE and I want to know why you are calling MY HUSBAND'S cell phone talking about can he drop his bio by your house. And what do you mean by all of this love you, miss you stuff," she screeched into the phone.

I thought, *'This can't be happening. This has got to be a joke!'*

"Excuse me!" I said - I didn't know what else to say at the moment.

"Listen, you strumpet, you better leave my husband alone. If I catch you near my husband again, I'm going to put my fist so far down your throat that I'm going to come out with an ankle," she snarled irately at this point.

Benita was looking down at me and I knew she could tell that I was upset. I couldn't stop the water from filling up in my eyes. "Listen, I *did not* know he was married. Had I known that he was married, I wouldn't have ever dealt with him," I said with a huge lump in my throat.

"What do you mean DEALT with him; all of you whores are the same. You knew he was married. He's a national

Evangelist. EVERYONE knows that he is married. But I tell you what, you got one more time to call his cell phone and I'm going to come down there and beat your ass," she said sounding anxious.

"You call yourself a First Lady talking like that? You should be directing your anger towards *him*, not me," I said now getting mad myself.

"I am a First Lady, because I am his WIFE and I'm not giving my husband up for you and the other hundred women that have tried," she yelled at the top of her lungs.

"You know you are pitiful, I feel sorry for you, but I assure you that you will not have to worry about KIYAH anymore," I said preparing myself to hang up.

"I feel sorry for YOU, cause when I catch you, I'm going to beat the living hell out of you," she said as I was hanging up the phone in her face.

"Kiyah, who was that?" Benita asked

"No one," I said while getting up and preparing to leave the office. I didn't want Benita to see me crying. As I was walking past Sandy's desk, she looked up at me and shook her head as I was entering the hallway. I heard the phone ringing and I heard Sandy yell into the phone in a closed mouth-teeth gritting tone, "Stop calling here you psychotic bitch!"

Once I reached the bathroom, I couldn't hold back the tears. *How could he lie to me? He was supposed to be a minister.* While I wiped my eyes and tried to get myself together, I noticed that

Sandy was standing in front of the door that lead into the bathroom as if she was guarding against anyone from coming inside.

"Sandy, what are you doing?" I asked between sniffles.

"Kiyah, I thought you might need some privacy, so I'm going to stand here until you get yourself together and make sure no one comes in," she said sympathetically.

Then she continued, "I know that this is hard for you Kiyah, because it was hard for me" as she lowered her eyes. Shocked, I stopped crying for a minute and asked, "What do you mean it was hard for *you*?"

"Maybe I should have told you this before, but you were just so unapproachable. And besides, at first out of animosity I thought it would feel good to see *you* hurt the way he hurt *me*."

What was she talking about? I couldn't understand. But something in the pit of my stomach told me I would understand a whole lot more in a few minutes.

Sandy continued, "You see, Kiyah, all of these years you were the lucky one. You got a rich daddy and your mother spoiled you to death while I had to sit around and wonder where my next meal was going to come from. Here you were being fed with a silver spoon and always having the best and I hated you for it. I hated you for the loving, close-knit family you have because I'm not close to my brothers and sisters. In fact, we don't even talk! I hated you more and more every time I saw you laughing with your sisters and brothers. Kiyah, I'm ashamed to say it but I was happy when you and your husband broke up and I rejoiced in your tears. I always saw you as a person who thought you were better than others. I was wrong. I need to apologize to you to free myself."

Sandy was now crying herself.

"You don't have to apologize Sandy because I was just as wrong. I always felt like I was an outcast. I was very insecure. It wasn't always easy for me being the pastor's daughter and it still isn't," I continued between tears.

"Yes, my family has a little money, but money could never replace the times I had to give my Christmas gifts away to people visiting over the holidays because my mother didn't want *them* to feel bad. Money could never replace the heartache I felt when I learned that my husband had used me for the money he thought my family had and conspired with his mistress to rob me of all of my worldly possessions. Money could never take away the pain I felt at seeing my mother losing limb after limb in the midst of her sickness and then seeing her lifeless body laid out in front of thousands of people on display.

You see, Sandy, all of my life I had to watch my parents live for the Church and even at home, they were working for the Church. Money could never replace the hurt I felt when they never made it to the games I cheered at, when they never attended any of the fashion shows I gave and when they never attended the talent shows I entered. They were too busy with the Church. So all of my life, I had to share my parents with the Church. I thought that I had gotten used to that idea, but at my mother's funeral, I just wanted that private time, that one moment with her alone, to tell her how much I loved her and how much I was going to miss her. I wanted to tell her that I was sorry for all the times I disappointed her and all the times I lied trying to get her attention. But I couldn't because there were so many people there. Even at her wake I didn't get to view her body before anyone else saw her. As I stood at the back of the church and saw her casket up in the front, I thought that at that very moment I would have given anything and traded positions with anyone in an instant," I said now sobbing.

Sandy had come over and put her arms around my shoulder. "Kiyah, I didn't know," Sandy said while consoling me. But, I wasn't finished telling her how I felt. I really had to get it all out, because everyone thinks that the Simmons family has it good, but we have been through hell and high water.

"Sandy, you may think we may I have it all, but my family has been through a lot. When I was fourteen years old and was coming home from a party at one of the local Catholic schools, I walked up on my porch and saw glass from our storm door shattered all over the porch. Walked in the house only to find that my older brother Vincent had been shot five times in front of our house. He lived but was paralyzed from the waist down. Do you know what it's like to see your brother one day walking and in a wheel chair the next? This took a great toll on my family. My brother is a very strong person and without his legs, he didn't want

to live. In the middle of the night he would scream "SOMEBODY
SHOOT ME, I DON'T WANT TO LIVE," he would holler,
"DADDY, MOMMY, WHY CAN'T I MOVE MY LEGS?
SOMEBODY HELP ME! It broke my heart night after night
hearing him scream in agony and not being able to do anything to
help him. I know my mother was heartbroken from it. This was her
child and she couldn't do anything to help him. The doctors said
they were spasm pains.

Shortly thereafter, my brother, the one that's two years
older than me, was slipped some bad drugs, which caused him to
lose his mind. He was practically a genius, and now look at him.
And it doesn't stop there; it never ends with my family, it's always
something. My mother taught us to love one another and stick
together through thick and thin. I guess God gave her that insight
because he knew that there was going to be many battles that we
would have to fight our way through," I said as I calmed down.

Sandy was still distraught. "Kiyah, I had no idea that you
have been through all of that. I am so sorry, really I am. I want
you to know that you're not the only one Leon has fooled," she
said, wiping away her tears.

"Sandy, what are you talking about? I was just talking
about my family, this has nothing to do with Leon. What are you
talking about?" I said trying not to sound totally confused.

"Kiyah, I knew a month ago when he called for you and sent the flowers. I knew you were dating Leon Booker. I recognized his voice," Sandy said, but I instantly interrupted her.

"Sandy, I'm not dating Le...," I tried to say, but she stopped me.

"Kiyah, please! You don't have to try and cover up. I know, Kiyah, because he did me the same way," Sandy said looking me straight in the eye. Then she continued, "Kiyah, the only difference between you and I was that I knew he was married and you didn't. A year ago, I was at a revival in New York and Leon was the guest speaker. Girl, he spoke with such power and conviction, that I was just in awe of his ability. I thought he was handsome, but I never expected my little attraction to go anywhere. As I was leaving the revival, one of his assistants met me outside while I was on my way to the car and told me that their pastor wanted me to meet him at the Folk's Diner in Hackensack. He said the Pastor had a Word for me and that I should come alone because what God was about to do for me was just for me. I dropped my girlfriend off in Teaneck and headed over to Hackensack. It took me all of forty minutes to reach the diner. When I got there, Leon was already there with one of his assistants. As I approached his table, the young man with him got up and went and sat at the front of the diner near the entrance. Once I sat down Leon began telling me how he noticed me looking at him while he was preaching and that his spirit told him that I was attracted to him and wanted him.

He cautioned me that he was a man of God and the Holy Spirit wouldn't lie to him. All along, I knew he was right. He told me that he was married and that his wife no longer satisfied him. He went on and on about how he was no longer attracted to her. To make a long story short, we went to the hotel that night and had sex and many more times after that over the course of a two to three month period. Leon treated me like a queen, bought me expensive things, he told me that he loved me and I thought he was God sent. Then suddenly a few days went by without him calling. When I finally decided to call him to see if anything was wrong, his number was changed. I was heartbroken, so the very next Sunday morning I went to his church and sat in the back. When he noticed me in the back he started preaching about how people were trying to ruin his life and right then and there I knew something was really wrong. But I never suspected that when I decided to walk up front of the church during his call to present a seed offering, that his wife would jump up in front of the whole congregation and start attacking me. She called me everything but a child of God and told me '*how dareI come into their church knowing that I was trying to destroy their family.*' I looked at Leon while the men in the church were separating us and all he did was turn his back to me. I ran out the building in tears. Later on through the rumor mill, I found out that, his wife had known about us and was spying on me. She had found out where I lived, where I worked and where I went to church. She had warned Leon that if he didn't stop seeing me and cut all ties with me that she was going to leave him." Sandy was now wiping the streams of tears that were now running down her cheeks.

"Sandy, you mean to tell me that you used to date Leon? But I just saw you at the service down at Bishop Johnson's church shouting and praising God as if nothing had ever happened between the two of you?" I asked.

"Yes you did, Kiyah, and I don't know what type of explanation you want for that. I love to hear him preach. For a while, I couldn't think of going to hear him preach, but now that I was over him, it doesn't bother me. The man can preach the Word, that's one thing I can't deny. But what he does to young women isn't right. Right before you Kiyah, it was Audrey Battle from Faith Deliverance on Ninth Avenue. I think it took her all of six weeks to find out about him, and she was devastated," Sandy said as she gained her composure back.

"WHAT? I don't believe this; how can I let him come preach at my church knowing what type of man he is," I said, with my head in my hands.

"Kiyah, you have to let him come and preach. Everyone is expecting him and I know that God is still going to bless that service," Sandy said, holding me by my shoulders.

"I don't know about all of this, Sandy. Do me a favor, please don't mention this to anyone; the men at the church are looking forward to Men's Day and the flyers are already out. I don't know what I'm going to do. I need to go and talk to Queen Bee," I said while standing up in an effort to leave.

"You don't have to worry about me Kiyah. Your secret is safe with me, besides I've told you mine. Do you know how many times I hear people talk about the time Leon's wife attacked a young lady at his church during morning service? All I do is laugh along with them in order to keep from crying. No one knows that was me, except the people that were there that day, and I don't know any of them personally. I've never told anyone this Kiyah, except you," she said with her head tilted down.

"Sandy, your secret is safe with me as well, so I guess neither one of us has anything to worry about," I said while giving her a warm hug. She hugged me back tightly. Strangely enough in the midst of everything that was said in the bathroom, I felt like I had made a new friend.

After Sandy and I talked for a half an hour more in the bathroom, I walked back through the office, grabbed my things and headed straight out the door. It took me only ten minutes to reach Queen's house. I knew she was going to be livid. But I had to tell her. As I was walking down her driveway and before I could reach her door, my private cell phone rang. It was Leon.

"Sweetheart, did my wife call you today at your job?" He had the nerve to ask.

"Yes, she did; I thought you said you weren't married?"

"What did she say to you?" he asked.

"She said that she was your wife and that if I ever came near you again she was going to do all sorts of threatening things to me," I replied.

Leon was laughing now. "Look, sweetheart don't worry about her, she's not going to touch a hair on your pretty head. I'm not going to let her do anything to my angel. Kiyah, you know you are my angel right?" he said.

I stopped midway up Queen Bee's driveway. I didn't want to go into her house while I was still on the phone with him. "Leon, are you married?" I demanded.

No sound came through the phone for at least a minute then he answered me "Yes Kiyah, I am," he said reluctantly.

"Why did you lie to me?" I said now crying.

"Kiyah, I love you and I never wanted to hurt you. Can we meet somewhere and talk?" he said sounding so apologetic.

"NO, I don't want to ever see you again," I screamed while hanging up the phone. Immediately, before I could take one-step towards the house he called back. I don't know why but I answered through my tears, "Hello."

"Kiyah, please, let me explain," he said pleading.

"No, there is nothing to explain. I'm hanging up," I said.

"Don't hang up. Wait, I need to explain this to you. If you won't meet with me would you at least give me two minutes to try and make this thing right," he said really begging. Now this I wanted to hear. Here he had lied to no end and he thought that in two minutes he could make it right? He ain't hardly that clever.

"All right you have two minutes that's all and then I'm hanging up," I said in my most irritated tone while giving in to his request.

"Thank you, first of all, Kiyah. Let me admit one thing to you, I am married. But I truly don't consider myself married because my wife and I don't even sleep together. We are together solely for the sake of our Church. I'm not going to lose everything I've worked so hard for by divorcing my wife. Secondly, I can explain this to any woman I want and still have them. So I'm not just trying to run a game on you, Kiyah, just to continue sleeping with you. I can have any woman I want and the majority of the time I do. Until I met you, Kiyah, I was satisfied with having women all over the world in every state and country that I traveled in; they understood that I was married and they respected my gift. They rolled with the punches. But when I met you for some reason I knew that if I told you I was married that you wouldn't go along with it. The first thing you asked me on our first date was whether or not I was married, but before that you said *you would consider going out with me, but there were a few things you needed to know first.* That was the key right there, Kiyah, you needed to know that first. Proverbs 31 speaks of a virtuous woman and how she's hard to find. Every woman I dealt with either knew I was married before hand or either they didn't bother to ask until after we were already acquainted. I know that you are rare and precious; the Bible says so. Now look, I'm not proud of my behavior, but hey I'm not happy at home and haven't been for years. My wife doesn't do if for me anymore. I've ventured outside of my marriage plenty of times with plenty of different women with no intentions of ever leaving my wife. But with you, a virtuous woman, I am willing to give it all up. I am willing to leave my wife if that's what it is going to take not to lose you, Kiyah," By now Leon was sounding so sincere.

"Leon, I can't do this right now. I need time to think," I quickly hung up the phone.

As I entered Queen Bee's back door Leon was calling again. However, I did not answer.

"QUEEN," I yelled trying to locate her whereabouts in the house.

"I'M IN THE DEN," she yelled back. After traveling through the kitchen and down the hall, I found her relaxed on the couch with her feet up watching television in her cozy den. "Kiyah, what are you doing up here? Something must be wrong," Queen said while pulling her feet down from the coffee table and sitting up.

"I don't think Leon should speak for Men's Day," I said with my head tilted down.

"Why not? Have you two had your first argument?" Queen asked almost smiling in her tone.

"More like our last," I replied. "Listen, I don't know how to tell you this but Leon is married. His wife called me today at work and threatened me. I don't know what to do," I said now with tears forming in my eyes. A serious look came over Queen's face.

"Have you talked to him yet?" Queen asked while helping me to sit down.

"Yes, I just got off the phone with him and he admitted it. He says that he is not in love with his wife and...."

Queen, now thoroughly pissed, interjected, "THEY ALL SAY THAT!"

"But Queen, I can't understand how he can be married, ministering and spending an enormous amount of time with me?"

"One thing you should already know, Kiyah, is a man will find time to do anything he wants to do," she said while snapping her head from side to side as only a Black woman knows how to do. "I don't care what kind of song and dance he gives you, YOU'RE NOT seeing him anymore. Lord, I don't know what I'm going to tell the men at the church, this is a MESS," Queen said while pacing the floor. "Are you all right?" She turned to me and asked.

"I'm a little shaken up but I will be fine. The thing that bothers and confuses me the most is the fact that he touches people when he speaks and they feel the presence of the Lord and behind all of that is nothing but lies. How can God use him? If God is using him, how can he be a liar, a manipulator and an adulterer? Didn't God say that he will not dwell in an unclean temple," I asked with tears falling down my face.

Queen didn't say a word even though I know she knew that I had more to say.

"How can he be a man of God and do the things he has done. I'm so confused because I've heard him preach and he is very powerful and people catch the Holy Ghost all over the place. People came back to the Lord. Others gave their lives to Christ for the first time. I don't understand. This just doesn't make sense to me anymore. All of my life I've been in the church and all my life I knew how church people were suppose to live and how they were suppose to carry themselves. Being in the church all of my life, Queen, I knew how to give God a good dance. I knew how to give him a good praise. I knew that when the organ hit that certain chord, the tambourines would playing, and the drums were in high gear that this was the time to give God a joyful praise. It felt good and I was told that I was praising Him for something I had not received yet. But now I can't even praise Him. After seeing the other side of the ministry and being in the company of the very people that used to have me jumping and shouting by the words that they were speaking from their mouths. These ministers, these same ministers, now turn my stomach. It's enough to almost question *religion period,* " I said in frustration.

"Now wait a minute, Kiyah, you must be losing your mind. I don't know what Leon has done to you but you better understand one thing. The Bible tells us that gifts come without repentance. Leon may be gifted and I'm sure he is, but if he doesn't repent and turn from his wicked ways he's going to wake up in hell one day. Everyone that he spoke God's Word to, if they received it and believed it and applied it to their lives, will make Heaven their home. One more thing you must understand is that God will not dwell in an unclean temple but he will *use* an unclean temple. God is going to deliver his Word to His people no matter what. Leon is just a messenger even if he doesn't take heed to the very words he preaches. He shall be a castaway," Queen said, now preaching a little bit herself.

"Now I want you to repent yourself while you still have a chance. I know that you've been disappointed by men in your life over and over again Kiyah. Understand that man will let you down every time. Why don't you try Jesus! Try Jesus Kiyah. I mean really try Jesus! He will work it out for you," Queen said while getting her Bible off the shelf that was built into her walls.

For the next two or three hours Queen was giving me scripture after scripture on the Word of God. St. John 1:1, in the beginning was the Word and the Word was with God and the Word was God. I started to understand that the Word of God is powerful all by itself. It doesn't matter who speaks it. It's going to accomplish what it was sent out to do and it will not return void.

The Word of God is powerful even in our prayers. The Bible says whatsoever we pray for and believe it we shall have it. God's Word is sharper than a two-edged sword; so no matter which way you slice it, it cuts deep. I was now getting a clearer understanding as to why the people were affected by Leon's preaching even though he wasn't living the way he should.

After studying with Queen for a while, I left to pick the kids up and after I got them home, I went up into my room. I wanted to study more on this Word. It's funny, I've heard most of these scriptures being quoted all of my life, but it seemed that they were taking on a new meaning to me. As I was reading, I learned that in order to understand the Word, I needed to understand God and the more I read up on God, I found out that I needed to understand Jesus. I was getting even more excited when I found David saying, "Oh taste and see that the Lord, He is Good and His mercy endureth forever," this was a relief to me. First of all, I love challenges. This was a challenge to me because every man that I've put my trust in lately had turned out to be anything but good for me. Secondly, this scripture was also telling me that I have mercy resting on my side. All I had to do was ask Him to forgive me for what I had done in my past and He would because His mercy endureth forever. I didn't have to feel ashamed anymore because of Jesus. He would wipe my slate clean as soon as I become Godly sorry; repent for what I had done and mean it with my heart.

As I was getting on my knees, my cell phone rang. It was Leon.

"Hello," I said.

"Kiyah, why haven't you been answering my calls?" he said sounding worried.

"Leon, you need to answer *your* call," I said very calmly.

"What do you mean?" he said confused.

"Leon, God has given you a gift to preach His Word with power and anointing, but you have used the very gift that He has given you to distort His people and you have turned it into a profitable business," I said. "Leon, you are more concerned about how much money you're going to make from preaching rather than how many souls you can win for the kingdom of God. Salvation is free, so who are you to make a mockery of that? God walked the earth and healed the sick, gave the blind their sight back, caused the lame to walk, raised people from the dead, and nowhere in there did He charge a fee. Yet you, you could receive nearly twenty thousand dollars for a single sermon and you complain and bicker. Jesus hung on a cross, nails in His hands and feet, pierced in His side for us to have a right to salvation and He never said a mumbling word. Paul traveled across the world and was jailed and eventually killed for preaching the Gospel of Jesus Christ and he felt indebted to those he couldn't get to. Did you hear me, Leon? He felt indebted to those he couldn't reach. Unlike you, you want people to go in debt cause you feel as though you can preach a little bit. Just as God gave you this gift, He can surely take it away. But you know what's even scarier, Leon; you can keep going on and on with what you're doing and you feel as though you're getting away with it because you're fooling the people. The sad part is that you *are* fooling the people, but the good part is that you're *not* fooling God. You're going to have to answer to God one day and if you don't change your wicked ways He's going to say *DEPART FROM ME, I KNOW YOU NOT*!" I was shocked that I was able to talk to him like this. But the Lord was bringing scriptures back to my remembrance one at a time in rapid succession.

Leon was quiet the whole time I spoke, and then he came back in a calm tone saying, "Kiyah that sounds cute. Now that you have spent some of that same money that you say I had no right to take; yet every time I reached in my pocket you had your hands open. Furthermore, you didn't fight the intimacy. If anything you encouraged it; always conveniently laying there with a towel on. Girl please! Now you want to preach to ME? You're no better than I was. I don't have to deal with this shit! If I want some ole holier-than-thou sanctified woman or somebody always trying to preach to me, I might as well stay with my wife," Leon said with such an arrogant tone. He almost made me curse, but you know what, just as he was finishing his statement, the Lord gave me peace. Instead of the feelings I was experiencing for him earlier, the ones that were filled with love and pain all at the same time, I now felt sorry for him because he had a form of Godliness; he looked the part, played the part and preached the part, but he was denying the power thereof. God is able to do above and beyond what we can ask or think. If Leon can raise himself a twenty thousand dollar offering, how much more would God do if he just trusted Him? Be faithful to God and he will pour you out a blessing that there shall not be room enough to receive. The Bible says that God will cause men to give into your bosom.

"Leon, you know what, I was wrong for sleeping with you. You are right about that. But you know what, I don't have to continue on in that way and God is able to restore me back to where I need to be. And you, Leon, you can also repent and make up your mind to serve God with your whole heart and He will bless your ministry even more. How can you preach His Word and not trust that he will do everything that He says He will do?" I said questioning him.

"Kiyah, you know what, you might make a good preacher one day yourself. You could really go places, make a whole lot of money," he said while laughing. Then he finished his statement by saying, "'cause you almost had me for a minute. If you continue with this foolishness I'm gonna have to hang up and try to locate someone with a more satisfying conversation," he said in a tone that lead me to believe that if I wasn't prepared to talk to him about us getting together, then he was no longer interested.

"Leon, you can do whatever you want to do, you disgust me," I said, angry now.

"Awe, that's just jealousy talking. Don't worry, Kiyah, I was just testing you. I'm not going to give your candy to anybody else, as long as you straighten up and act right," he said with that satisfied tone he gets when things are working out the way he wants them to.

"Yes, Leon, that's exactly what I'm going to do. I'm going straighten up and act right, starting now," I said as I proceeded to hang up the phone.

I got down on my knees and I prayed. *'I've heard people testify for years about what God has done for them and I've seen people shout and scream all over the sanctuary because they had received a blessing from God. I have seen people break down and cry because God has delivered them out of something. But now, Lord, I need deliverance. Father I want to experience You for myself. I need an experience with You right now, God. Father, in the name of Jesus please forgive me for all of my sins; I need to feel Your presence in my life, Lord God. I need to be restored back to a place of truth and I know that You are the truth and the light and that if I get back in your will, I will be able to see the right way I should go. I need to make a change in my life, Lord starting today and I can only do it with your help...'*

Sunday Morning, Men's Day

The kids had stayed home this weekend instead of going to their father's house. It was really fun having them home for a change on the weekend. It was a very strange yet wonderful feeling walking into the church on this Sunday morning with my kids in tow. We never went to church together. Normally their father would drop them off after they had stayed the weekend with him. I allowed them to go every weekend and instead of getting them on Saturday night, I would let them stay so that I could spend more time with Leon.

But today was a new beginning for us in so many different ways. I just felt like I was right on the edge of a breakthrough. It was hard for me to walk into church that morning, and part of me needed their support. All weekend long, I was reading my Bible and praying. Leon called several times but I did not answer. He left messages asking whether or not he should come and speak for our Men's Day service. I never responded. Queen and I decided to keep this whole ordeal private. I felt so ashamed and I didn't know who knew about this whole thing and who didn't. I really didn't want to go back to church and face everyone. But Queen told me I was just being silly, that no one was concentrating on my personal life. Yet in my heart I felt like the minute I stepped in the church that there was going to be a microscope on me.

The men at our church were still expecting Leon to come. I truly didn't know if he was going to come or not. I prayed and I prayed for God to let His will be done. I really didn't know how I was going to feel if he did come. I felt like everyone knew and I was so ashamed. I still had feelings for him yet none of them included respect. It's really weird to experience love and loss mixed with deceit and pity all at the same time. I was crazy in love with him and after learning of his deceit; I lost so much respect for him. Yet at the same time I felt sorry for him because he was fueling his plane for a one-way trip to hell.

As Kyasia, Kaseem and myself were walking into the church we could hear the praise team singing from the entrance of the building. Chills went down my spine as Brother Jeff from the praise team was belting out the words of "STAND" by Donnie McClurkin......*'What do you do, when you've done all you can, and it seems like it's never enough and what do you say when your friends turn away and you're all alone...Well, you just stand when there's nothing else to do, watch the Lord see you through.'*

I must have heard this song at least a thousand times. But today it seemed so different and new. I felt like everything was coming to a head. All of the pain over the last two years was closing in on me. I had prayed all weekend long for an answer from God and my heart was breaking because I didn't know what else to do. The last thing I needed to hear was this song. So as we entered the sanctuary I sucked in my breath to keep from crying and we walked over to the left side of the church where my family normally sat. Everyone was so embellished in their praise, that they did not even see us enter. While the kids sat and I remained standing. Queen was standing and waving her hands with tears streaming down her face. This was her way of praising God. When she felt my presence, she reached over and held my hand. She knew what I was going through. I didn't know how much more of this I could take.

Daddy was sitting in the pulpit listening to the praise team. Every now and then he would stomp his feet and say "Yes, Lord!" The praise team continued to back Brother Jeff up as he continued to the next verse. *'What do you give when you've given your all and it seems like you can't make it through, well you just stand when there's nothing left to do, you just stand."* Brother Jeff was singing from his heart and I felt an urgency building up in my spirit. There was a sweet spirit in the place that morning and as I looked around and saw so many people crying I knew that, I wasn't the only one that was going through something. When Ever-Ready came in, she came up and stood beside Queen and I. She immediately took my other hand and just held it, squeezing it every now and then. She only said four words to me. The tears started flooding down her face. "Are you okay, Kiyah," she said through whimpers.

As Brother Jeff proceeded to the next verse, I could no longer suppress the anguish burning in my heart. He belted out *'Tell me how do you handle the guilt of your past? Tell me how do you deal with the shame and how can you smile when your heart*

201

has been broken and filled with pain? *HOLD ON, THROUGH THE STORM, STAND THROUGH THE RAIN, THROUGH THE PAIN, HOLD ON, JUST BE STILL, AFTER YOU'VE GONE THROUGH THE HURT, PRAYED AND CRIED, PRAYED AND YOU'VE CRIED, AFTER YOU DONE ALL YOU CAN, JUST STAND.'*

I couldn't help but to breakdown thinking about the past two years of my life. All we did taking care of our mother. We took care of her around the clock, yet in all we did, God still saw fit to call her home. After all, I did to make my husband happy; working two jobs, giving him all my money, standing behind him even when I knew he was wrong, yet he still never appreciated me the way he should've. Now with Leon, he was so persistent in rushing me into a relationship with him. Once I finally gave in and fell in love with him, I come to find out that he was just lying and deceiving me the whole time. I threw my hands up to break loose from my sisters, so that I could clutch my heart because the pain was choking me, and as I did I yelled, "Jesus!!!" letting it all out.

Bent over I continued to cry, "Jesus!" Every time I called on Jesus, I could hear my sisters say it right after me. "Jesus!" they said. The ushers came over to help me but Queen told them to leave me and that I would be okay. I continued to call out "Jesus!" as loud as I could. "Jesus!" I needed to feel normal again, I needed all of this hurting to go away.

Before I knew it, most of the people in the sanctuary were helping me to call on the name of the Lord. "Jesus, Jesus, Jesus!" By this time, Daddy and my brother Jared were down from the pulpit laying hands on me and as they prayed, I felt the presence of God all over me. While they were praying for me, I heard the Lord speaking to me: '*Kiyah, why are you calling Me like you're waiting for Me to come and answer you? I've been here all the time, waiting on you. I'm here, Kiyah, I've always been here waiting for you to surrender and just say YES.*' The voice was unlike any voice I had ever heard before yet it had a familiar tone. It was neither a male's voice nor a female's voice yet it was a human voice. It was peaceful and profound at the same time.

I started screaming and shaking because I was scared and happy all at the same time. My sisters were trying to hold me, but I couldn't be contained. The voice continued, "*Say yes to My will and to my way. Then you may cast ALL your cares upon me and I will give you rest.*" As I began to say, *Yes Lord, Yes Lord* over and over again, I knew that my breakthrough was coming. I began to praise God with my whole heart and once I stopped shouting and dancing, I realized that God had given me a new praise. He had given me a praise of declaring victory in the midst of my battle.

Once I sat down and started rocking myself back and forth to calm down, Queen started fanning me and Ever-Ready was handing me Kleenexes to wipe my face off. I just kept thanking Jesus. When I finally calmed completely down, I noticed that people in all different parts of the sanctuary were laid out on the floor crying and yelling out to God. There was a move of the Holy Spirit in this place. I wanted to tell Queen and Ever-Ready how God had revealed things to me while I was in the spirit. But before I could I saw Leon and his entourage enter the sanctuary. As they walked down the center aisle, Leon and Paul walked straight up into the pulpit and the others sat on the front row. Immediately, I started to cry. I didn't know why but I needed to get out of there. Queen tried to stop me, but I insisted on leaving. I assured her that I would be right back. As I got up and walked out of the sanctuary, I felt Leon looking at me but I didn't look back at him. It seemed as though I couldn't breathe until I got out of that room.

I went straight to the ladies room. I went into the first stall and let the tears flow. After a minute I helped myself to some of the tissue to wipe my face and proceeded to come out only to find Sandy standing there waiting for me. "Kiyah, are you okay," Sandy said holding her hand out.

As I grabbed her hand, I said, "I'll be fine."

"Why don't we go outside and get you some air," Sandy suggested.

"No, I better go back inside. My sisters will worry if I don't come back soon," I replied.

"Come on, girl, there's at least a thousand people inside that room. They are not going to miss you," Sandy said pulling me outside the bathroom. As we were walking out the ladies room, which was right across from the men 's room, we ran smack dead into Miles.

"Miles!" I said in a voice of shock.

"Kiyah, I was just inside looking for you," he said while grabbing my hand. Miles was looking sharp, he had on a black suit and it fit him nicely. He looked very nice all dressed up.

"Whatever message Leon wants to send through you, Miles, keep it, I don't want to hear it," I said putting up my hands.

Sandy was looking at Miles and then looking at me. I could tell she was admiring him and trying to add up all sorts of things in her head. So I decided to introduce them. "Miles, this is Sandy, she works with me. Sandy, this is Miles, he works with Leon," I said.

"Not anymore," Miles said. "Look, I don't want to be rude, Ms. Sandy, but if you don't mind could I speak to Kiyah alone please," he said in a very serious tone.

Sandy looked at me with her eyebrows raised and said, "Sure, but I will be back out shortly to check on you, girlfriend" and walked away.

Once Sandy left, Miles asked me to walk outside with him. After we got outside Miles turned to me and said, "Are you okay, Kiyah?" looking me straight in the eye.

"No, Miles, I'm not okay, but I'm better. I'll be all right." I knew that Miles knew what was going on. Somehow, I began to understand that he always knew that things were going to turn out this way.

"Listen, I'm here if you need someone to talk to. I don't work for him anymore, Kiyah. I had to quit after I got wind of what he did to you. Don't get me wrong; I'm not surprised that you found out about his wife. I knew eventually you would, but I never thought that he would have the nerve to come here and speak after all he's done to you. He's too damn cocky for me!" Miles said pacing back and forth.

"Well, Miles, I never told him not to come, but I just don't want to hear him speak. Miles, this might seem weird to you but the people are going to still be blessed by the Word of God even if Leon is the one that's speaking it," I said grabbing Miles arm to stop him from pacing.

"Kiyah, what are you talking about? You know the man is a liar and no good. What makes you think that people are going to blessed by a man like that," Miles said sounding very frustrated.

"That's my point, Miles, they won't be blessed by a man like that or blessed by a man period. The people will be blessed by the Word of God, so God is doing the blessing because the Word is God. No man can bless you, only God can bless you," I said.

"I don't know what your talking about, Kiyah" Miles answered.

"Think about it this way, Miles: a paperboy delivers the paper to many houses on his route. In that paper are many articles of which none of them he wrote. Yet he is the means by which the author of those articles will reach some of the readers," I said while visualizing it in my head.

Miles was looking at me in deep thought. I continued, "You see, Miles, he is just a messenger, a paperboy. People need to stop looking at the messenger and hear the message," I said now smiling, because I had realized that I had just ministered to myself.

Then Miles asked, "That sounds good, Kiyah, but if that is the case then why aren't you in there listening to him?"

A sense of peace came over me as Miles asked that question.

"I was thinking the same thing. I am going to go back in there now, but I would feel even better if you would come with me," I said extending my hand to Miles.

"I don't know if I could, Kiyah, I don't feel good about that brother and I don't want to go in there and pretend," Miles said pulling back.

"Don't pretend, Miles, because you don't have to. This doesn't have anything to do with Leon. It's about God. Listen to his Word and receive it," I said while pulling him towards the sanctuary.

When I finally got Miles into the sanctuary, Leon was more than half way through his sermon and the people were praising God already. Miles held my hand and from time to time, he would look over at me. I could tell that Leon was very angry by seeing

Miles and I together, because he started preaching about how the people closest to you and even family will back stab you and work against you. Leon was a mess, using that pulpit for his own personal gain every chance he got. Leon finished preaching approximately fifteen minutes after Miles and I walked in.

Afterward the men led him out and into the back office where he could change and be comfortable. Sandy, Miles and I were in the sanctuary talking after service had let out when Brother Hutch, the President of the Men's Auxiliary at my church, came up to me and said that Leon wanted to see me in the back before he left. Shocked, I turned to Brother Hutch and nervously asked, "Why? Why would he need to see me before he leaves?"

Brother Hutch just smiled and said, "I don't know, Sister Kiyah. He said you invited him to speak for us today and he wanted to meet you so that he could thank you personally for your invitation. So if you would come with me, I will take you back to where he is." He extended his hand out to lead me towards the back.

I looked at Miles and Sandy then I turned to Brother Hutch and gave in by saying, "Sure, no problem, which way?"

He led me through the back stairway and over to the new offices that were built with bathrooms and studies attached. Leon was sitting when I got back there. The moment he saw me he stood up. He was alone. The other guys were in another room. Brother Hutch immediately left after escorting me into the office.

Leon stared at me for a moment before speaking. "I assume that you will be returning my phone, since you can't answer my calls. There's no need for you to have it," he said standing within inches of me.

"No problem," I said with no emotion.

"Also, the credit cards I gave you, rip them up because I will be closing the accounts," he said while running it down to me, "you won't be running around spending my money with some other nigga," he said as he finished his statement in an angry tone.

"Okay," I repeated with no emotion.

"You call yourself getting back at me by being with my no good cousin and then throwing it all up in my face. No wonder he quit - he could no longer face me like a man. I always knew he wanted you, Kiyah. I knew it," Leon said with a snarl.

"First of all, Leon, I was not with Miles. We are just friends. This is the first time I've seen Miles since he helped me with my luggage at the airport," I said.

"Whatever, Kiyah, it doesn't matter anymore," Leon said stopping me with his 'talk-to-the-hand motion in my face.

Coldly I look at him and said, "you're right, it doesn't matter. I've got to go and I will be praying for you, Leon." I turned and made my way to the door.

"Kiyah!" Leon said as I was walking out.

"What, Leon, what is it?" I asked, now a little frustrated.

"I'm sorry, Kiyah, I'm really sorry for hurting you," Leon said looking me straight in the eye. All I could do was look at him. Then I walked out.

Leon never came or called for his phone. I didn't think he would. Miles and I talk all the time and eventually he became like a big brother to me. Sometimes I wondered if he wanted more out of our friendship, but I guess he sensed that I didn't and just never tried. Sandy and I are still working on getting him saved.

As for Leon, he's still up to no good. Just last week rumors were floating all around about him and yet another young lady. A singer from Newark..........Now *that's* another story...........